CEO & Hustlers
Business Matters

A NOVEL BY

Nola Jewels

Synopsis

The Fields sisters are the true definition of a triple threat. They are intelligent, beautiful and successful in their life and careers. Even with all their success and talent, something is missing from their lives. Karman the oldest, is a successful Commercial Real Estate agent flying high at the top of her game. Her career is the love of her life right now. The more she achieves in her career, the more she craves success and she will stop at nothing to continue her rise to the top. When a bump in the road appears in the form of Legend, she faces a crossroads in her life. Legend is walking temptation. He is street, crazy, loud and far from her type. His lifestyle and hardcore antics could cast a shadow on everything she's worked hard to obtain. Even someone as successful as Karman has to know all work with no play can't be real life.

Bella Fields has a complicated lifestyle. She enjoys control and uses it as a weapon to protect herself. She uses control at work, at home and even in the bedroom. Especially in the bedroom. When Bella meets Aspen the sparks fly. Aspen is exactly Bella's type with one exception, he's uncontrollable. He wants to run the show causing Bella to come face to face with her lifestyle, choices and her need to control everything and everyone. When the control she has starts slipping through her fingers she doesn't know what to do. Can she exist without the one thing that has protected her for so long?

Last is Journi Fields. Journi doesn't want the career, success or the control. She only wants love. Her current relationship is giving her the exact opposite. On a weekend trip, heartbroken and alone she meets Mecca. Mecca is everything she's ever wanted or needed in a man. They fall fast in love with one another. It seems like the perfect romance until her secrets and his secrets collide and combine to make the perfect storm of trouble.

These three sisters thought they had everything figured out: life, love and their careers. That is until their world is turned upside down. They're about to learn the difference between a CEO and Hustler and why it counts when its matters of the heart. Nothing is just a business matter.

Chapter 1

Settling

Journi Fields

Alexa play. . .Summer Walker. . .Settling

I hear my name come across the intercom and I cringe. Walking toward the office I attempt to calm my nerves. Maybe it's not bad news, maybe they just need me to cover another class. Who am I kidding that would be bad news too. I'm already substituting for the math class and the history class, which is crazy because I teach English, creative arts and dance. I walk in the office and the snobby secretary looks me up and down and tells me to take a seat. I roll my eyes and I sit down. I can't stand her ass. Hell, I feel the same way about most of the people at this school. I thought working for a private school would be different. But I'll take public school any day of the week. Sure, the resources were short and non-existent, but the kids were nice and respectful. Even the other teachers and staff were friendly. I would run across a few that were complete assholes but for the most part my experiences were always good. My sister told me not to come to this bougie ass private school. Since I've been here, I've been called to the office six times. Either I wasn't allowing *little Jimmy* to get away with being a brat or one of those fat ass moms was complaining about my outfit.

Mr. O'Conner, the principal, steps out his office and motions for me. "Ms. Fields, please come into my office."

He takes a seat in the chair behind his desk and I take the chair opposite of him. His office reeks of cheese. Old nasty funky aged cheese. I always want to bring air fresher in here with me or at least gift him a plug in. "You needed to see me." I want to get right to the point. I don't have time to sit here with this pervert. I feel like he's already undressed me with those little beaded eyes of his.

"I like you Ms. Fields. Most of the kids and the parents like you too. You're a good teacher and what you've done in the dance class is nothing short of amazing. I haven't seen those kids dance that good in my whole career here with the school."

He clears his throat. I use this as my time to speak. "Thank you, Mr. O'Conner, I enjoy working at the school. I think the resources here at this school are exceptional. I'm looking forward to teaching the kids the spring dance and showcasing it at the spring recital."

"I was looking forward to it as well. However, I received a call from the school's board members this morning. They are cutting the funding for the Arts department. I'm sorry Ms. Field but your services will no longer be needed."

"Are you serious?" I was in shock. Public schools cut funding for their arts programs all the time. Not private schools. I notice he wasn't making eye contact with me. He was fumbling with his pen. Since there's a shortage of teachers they still need me. Something else was going on. "Tell me the truth. This school has endless funds. Plus, you need me to fill in the spots for the classes with no teacher."

"You're right about the funding but we want to ensure we keep it."

"I'm not sure I understand."

"It seems as if you've caught the eye of a certain board member's husband. She was extremely excited her husband was finally taking an active role in their daughter's education only to find out he was staying in the evening just to watch you dance. Once he realized you were teaching her math class, he also began dropping her off in the morning. Using it as another opportunity to see you. And for you both to be together again. At least that's the story his wife told the board. She went to them and accused you of having an affair with her husband. The board doesn't want any scandals at the school. They've decided to let you go quietly."

"Affair? Are you kidding me? I'm not sleeping with anyone's husband. Especially not him." I knew exactly who he was talking about. Jennifer's dad. He was always complimenting me on my outfits and my hair. I had to stop him from hugging me on more than one occasion. I would extend my hand to him instead. "Mr. O'Conner, I need my job. I can't help it if a parent has an attraction to me. I always make sure I'm polite and I don't return any of the advances. Maybe I can transfer to another class or we can move the student to a different teacher."

"It's already done. You don't understand the power and money she has. She wants you gone, so you're gone."

"Just like that? No investigation? No one asking me if it's true or not?"

"It doesn't matter if it happened or didn't happen. The decision has been made. They have asked that you leave. You'll be paid for the remainder of the semester. I really am sorry."

"I'll sue this damn school."

"On what basis? Everything I've told you is off the record. Your termination papers simply state funding cuts. Take the money and go peacefully Ms. Fields. I'll make sure to give you a good recommendation. Don't ruin your chances of working at another private schools. If you make trouble, they will talk and blackball you. Preventing you from working in any school system out here in Atlanta. Hell, even Georgia. I've seen them do it. You're a nice young woman who has a long, full career ahead of her. Just go."

His statement was final. He gets up from his seat and walks over to the door to open it for me. I can't believe someone would get upset with me for something her husband is doing. I'm not interested in any of these married men. None of these men at all. Most of them are old and white. I walk out the door, back to the area where the snobby secretary reaches down on the floor and comes back up with a box in her hand. She slaps it on the counter with a smirk on her face. I take it and toss it at her head. I want to go back and punch that smirk right off her face. I can't stand a jealous woman. If she wore a little make-up and did something to that rat's nest on her head, she might attract some attention herself. Who am I kidding, she's ugly there's just no helping that at all.

I pack my desk and leave before the end of the school day. It doesn't make any sense to stay and give the other teachers something else to talk about. I drive back to the townhouse I share with my boyfriend Bayden. To my surprise his car is already here. When I walk inside, he's sitting on the sofa on a call. The door dings alerting him of my presence. He turns and glances at me, gives me a funny look and drops his phone. He picks his phone back up and starts talking too low for me to hear the conversation he's having. I look at him. "Hey, I didn't expect you home. Is everything good?"

"Yeah. Its work give me a minute."

Work my ass. Not from that look on his face. "We need to talk. I'll be in the room when you're done." If I wasn't so angry from work, I would've addressed the elephant in the room. Or perhaps if I gave a fuck, I would have questioned him. I could give two fucks about who he's talking to now. I'm not a jealous or insecure woman. Either you want me, or you don't. It's that simple. I've learned the truth always comes to light. And with Bayden the truth always comes out in some form. Let's see the last time it was an STD that was not really his fault, *it just kind of happened*. His words not mine. And that time I found underwear in our bed that weren't mine. And who can forget the used condom I found on the back seat of his car. If he is cheating again, which by the hush tone he was speaking in, that's it. My thoughts are broken when he enters the room.

"You're home early. What's wrong?"

I tell him everything that happened. "I just can't believe they would rather fire me than address her husband coming up to the school."

"I told you to stop wearing those tight ass outfits to school. You need to learn to dress more conservative."

"Are you really trying to blame me too?"

"I'm not blaming you. I'm just saying you had a job at a very prestige school not one of those hood schools. You have to learn to dress the part. Listen, if you work in my office there's a dress code. Don't think the women in my office aren't shapely. Because some of them are downright fine. They just know how to hide it better. If you want to get to that level, you need to learn how to do the same thing."

"Hiding my figure is not my goal. Teaching my students is my goal."

"Dressing professional leads to a better job. It could rescue you from the hassle of those bad` ass kids. You could teach on the corporate level. But you'll be required to learn how to dress."

He heard nothing I said. "Getting a corporate job is not my goal."

"You should really think about it. You know put that degree of yours to work. This is what the sixth or seventh school you've worked at. Don't you think it's time for a change? You know time to get a big girl job with actual benefits and 401K pl for the future. Not just grading papers, playing in paint and dancing all day."

"Wow Bayden. Just wow. I know I'm not making six figures like you, but I do work a real job. I love teaching. And for your information it is real work. Also, I could go to work in a sheet, and it won't stop my ass from being seen." I turn to walk out the door and he stops me.

"You're angry. Let's not talk about this right now. Just relax. I wasn't trying to offend you. I was just making some suggestions. You know I love this ass of yours."

His hands are roaming my body and he's kissing my neck. "Bayden."

"Let me make you feel good baby. Just relax."

Ten minutes later my legs were starting to shake and not in a good way. I wouldn't complain if it was in a good way. In fact, I would welcome the pain. They were shaking because I could feel them starting to ache and about to go numb. I can't hold this position much longer. Bayden has been between my legs for the last ten minutes and he has yet to find my spot, the spot or any damn spot. I know I had dried up eight minutes ago, but he was still going. He was moaning more than me. I guess he was enjoying himself. When I see his head pop up, I let out a sigh of relief.

"That's what you needed. A little love from daddy."

Bayden's eyes are wild like he's a beast and I was his supper. I want to tell him nothing he's done has made me feel any better, but I don't because I'm exhausted with trying to get my point across to people today.

He and I have been dating for about two years. He was the perfect guy on paper. Unfortunately, none of his paper perfection transferred over to the real world. Of course, when we first started dating, he was caring, supportive, smart and successful. He was everything a girl could want except in the bedroom. I figured in time I could teach him how to do a few things. How to please my body. He handles the bedroom the same way he handles his job, fast and uncaring. I take that back. He handles his job much better. He's calculating and meticulous at his job. In the bed with me he can be boring and predicable. I know what he's going to do before he even does it. Like right now. He's going to tell me to turn over, he'll give me a few pumps, talk some shit and cum in a matters of seconds. It's always the same.

"Turn over."

I knew it. I peep for the condom first. I don't take any more chance with him. I told him my birth control pills were making me sick. He doesn't want kids, which made it easy for him to agree to using condoms. I turn over and he does his best at giving me what he considers pleasure. I don't even bother to pretend like I'm enjoying myself. When I feel him jerk, I know it's over. He has the nerve to be breathing hard like he really did something. "Let me get a towel." I rush off to the bathroom, just to save face. Today I just can't hide my disappointment. Not today. I was already a ball of emotions before, this was like putting a cherry on top of all the other things in my life that was out of order. I didn't want to cry. I've already cried three times today. It was the anniversary of my mother's death. On top of that losing my job. I just want the pain to go away. I just want him to comfort me and make me feel better. Not judge me for my career choice and my clothing. Thinking about my mom, I'm reminded of the last conversation she and I had together before she passed. She asked me if I was truly happy. Deep down I knew I wasn't but instead of speaking the truth I smiled and assured her I was more than happy. It was a lie last year and it's a lie right now.

My mom couldn't stand Bayden. His perfect persona didn't fool her. She saw right through the façade. Every day I'm with him I'm seeing right through it too. Bayden is the all-American guy you see standing in the room wearing the three-piece designer suit and the smile. He's 6'2 with a beautiful honey-mustard complexion that surrounds this slender frame. He graduated top of his class at Morehouse and worked his way up in less than five years' time to a cozy VP spot at an advertising agency. He's the man who makes things happen in the boardroom and commands attention in and out of the office. He's charming and good looking and powerful. All the things that attracted me to him. All the things that were now turning me off about him. He was demanding of my time, causing me to adjust my schedule to his busy work schedule. I made sure I was available when he wanted and needed me. In the process I was losing myself. I was so busy supporting him and his rise to fame, I was watching my dreams fade into I should've, would've and could've. I thought if I gave him time, he would settle a little bit into his career and then I could settle into mine. Now it seems like I'm the one that's settling.

I was trying to wash my face, but his iPad was in the way. I swear he leaves this thing everywhere. When I move it, a notification pops up from someone name Lushlips69. It says ***can't wait to see you at home tonight. This weekend will be everything***

we dreamed. I can't say that I'm shocked. I knew it, I felt it in my body. Every random time he disappeared or was texting someone all hours of the night. *At home tonight?* The only thing that was surprising me was the word home. This is home. Our home. And this weekend? This weekend we have plans to attend my cousin's birthday party. I look around the bathroom and notice his bag with all his grooming stuff is packed and on the side. It's only Wednesday, he doesn't need to pack this early. He's cancelling on me again and this time it's for some bitch he playing house with. Of all days for him to do this he does it today. Not today. I just can't handle it today. I walk out the bathroom and he was walking around putting his clothes in a suitcase. "Bayden, it's a little early to pack, isn't it." I was repeating stay calm in my mind over and over.

"I was going to call you earlier and let you know something came up for work and I need to go out of town and meet with a client."

"A client for work? We have plans."

"Baby it's work. It's not like it's a pleasure trip. I don't have a choice."

He has the balls to actually look me in my face and lie to me. I can't believe this shit. "You have a choice. You always have a choice. We have plans this weekend. You promised you would come. It's my cousin's birthday."

"Listen, it's work. Besides you and I both know how this birthday celebration will end."

"And how is that?"

"You know your family is ghetto as hell. Someone will probably end up fighting or shooting somebody. But that's neither here nor there. It's work baby. Let me take my shower. I have a flight to catch."

I watch him walk into the bathroom and I can hear the shower running. I start pacing the floor. I want to fight his ass just thinking about all the shit he does to me. I want to kill him just off the shit he's said to me today. Instead I pick up the phone and text my sisters. When he walks out the bathroom, I'm sitting on the bed with my arms folded.

"I don't have time to do this shit again with you today. I will not keep repeating to you how important my career is to me." He shakes his head and buttons the last button on his shirt. He grabs his keys off my dresser and starts walking toward the door. "Journi you know how I feel about you. I've shown you over and over. I'll text you when I have some free time."

I watch him walk out the door. I know exactly how he feels about me. He's shown me more than once. When someone shows you who they are you have to believe them. I was to blind to see what he was showing me. To blind to realize he was playing me. Yeah, I could have questioned him about his infidelities, but he would only lie. I could have fought with him to stay but who wants someone they have to fight with to get them to love them. After all, is that even love? The doorbell rings breaking my thoughts. I open the door and my sisters are standing there dressed in black like they're about to commit a crime and don't want to get caught. I hug both of them and let them in. I swear Bella and Karman are the best sisters. They stay ready for anything. "I'm glad to see you guys. But one question why are you dressed all in black?"

Bella looks at me with a serious face. "Just in case you decided to kill his bougie ass. You know in case we need to move a body or something."

I can't help but to crack up laughing and Karman joins me. "Really?"

"I told her crazy ass; she watches too much tv. What happened this time, baby girl?" Karman walks in and takes a seat.

"What didn't happen today? I got fired from my job because some old ass man's wife wasn't feeling the fact, he was into me. Instead of her checking him she decides I need to go. That's not it though. I find out Bayden is cheating on me and ditching me to go hang out with Lushlips69. Get this part, they are hanging out at, *their home*. On top of all of that I miss mom and I just want to run to her right now and tell her she was right about his ass and get her advice or just get her to hug me and say it will be ok." I break down. Today has been emotionally draining. I was exhausted with trying to hold it together.

Karman takes a seat next to me and takes my hand. "Aww baby girl. How many times did we tell you Bayden's ass wasn't shit? And don't worry about that damn job, it wasn't right for you. It was taking away from your creativity. You need something that will let you express yourself."

"Karman is right. That job was not right for you. You were miserable all the time going there. And Bayden, don't let me get started on his ass. Fuck his tight suit wearing ass. Any man who can't be there for you on your bad days doesn't deserve you on your good days. Besides his suit so fucking tight it probably squeezed all the emotion out of his ass."

Only Bella could have me cracking up and crying at the same time. "I just thought all the times I've dropped everything for him, he would see it and return it."

Karman shakes her head, "That's your first mistake. You made yourself available to him every time he wanted you there.

You can't just drop everything you're doing for a man. He's not your husband. He's your boyfriend that's proven over and over that he's not shit."

"You're right Karman. I just thought, hell I don't know what I was thinking."

Bella looks at me with a serious face. "You was thinking with your eyes."

"Bella, don't do that."

"No Karm, we sugar coat shit for her all the time. She needs to hear this. Baby girl we love you, but you picked Bayden because he was good and clean cut and to you that translated to perfection. He made it easy for you stacking your account with money, taking you on trips and showing you the world. The truth is those trips were business trips. You were a prop for him. You know arm candy. And that money came at a price. He was paying for you to forget how rude and uncaring he really is. Paying for you to forget about him cheating on you every chance he gets."

Bella doesn't have a filter. She gives it to raw and straight forward. She never hid her dislike of Bayden. Her and mom were one in the same. They couldn't stand him. I didn't feel like arm candy. *Was I arm candy?* "I don't think I'm arm candy. I just feel like I've sat around waiting on him to change. The more I wait the more insensitive he becomes. This morning when I woke up, I was thinking about mom. Do you know he had the nerve to say that I need to just deal with it? That death is a part of life and I need to understand it and stop acting so damn childish."

"That's not him being insensitive Journi. That's him not giving a fuck. You've been wearing blinders when it comes to him. Bella is absolutely correct about everything she said. You're so busy trying to be a picture-perfect couple you don't even realize how much you've just settled for mediocre. Mediocre is actually giving it an upgrade. You settled into a role of the good girlfriend. You know the one who doesn't make a fuss about anything. Like tonight did you confront him about cheating?"

"There was really no need." I watch them both throw their hands in the air and yell out come on Journi. "Like I said, there was no need to cut up or clown. I'm over it. I called you both over to help me with my stuff." I point to the hallway at the packed suitcases and full boxes. "I just want to move on with my life."

"Wait a minute, you called us to be movers and not to give you good advice?" Bella was too out done.

Karman hugs me. "I'm proud of you. I thought we were going to have to drag you out of here. You let us do all that damn talking."

"Please you know how you like preaching to me. But I got it this time. When he gets back, I won't be here waiting on his ass. And I've already blocked him so he can't call me either."

"You sure you don't want to break something. Mess this place up a little bit."

"Nah, Bella I'm good. Let's just go. I don't hate him. I just don't want him anymore." Although I would never say it out loud. A little part of me wants him to get his shit together so I can come back. As I close the door, it hits me like a ton of bricks. He's never going to get it together and he'll never love me the right way. A sadness starts to set in me. I wasted all my time and energy on the possibility of a successful relationship that would someday turn into a marriage complete with kids and the white picket fence. All for it to end with me walking away with nothing. Not even a whole part of myself. Just a shell of who I used to be.

Chapter 2

Playing Games

Bayden McMichael

Alexa play . . . Chris Brown. . . No Guidance

I didn't care about Journi getting angry with me. Journi is a beautiful woman and smart when she puts her mind to it. She's just all over the place. I'm sick of trying to center her and get her going in the right direction. When she and I met that first night I was taken back by her beauty and her body. But I was more impressed with how my clients were awestruck by her. My company was sponsoring an art exhibit with a group of artist from the area. The tickets sold out in minutes. The clients were tremendously pleased with the turn out and the exhibit. So pleased, they were considering doing the showcase on a quarterly basis. That meant big bucks for me and more money in my pocket. I was excited until they started questioning me about some of the art pieces. I didn't have a clue about the artist or the pictures. Art is not my thing. I'm a businessman. I was stumbling over my words when Journi stepped beside me looking stunning and started explaining in great detail the name of the artist and the work the client was questioning. When the client walked away, she whispered to me, ***you looked like you needed a little help***. I asked her to accompany me the remainder of the night. She did the perfect job of answering all the questions and explaining everything. The result was me getting my client to agree to signing for a quarterly art exhibit. A two million dollar agreement. I was in awe of how easy Journi was able to get me more money on top of more money. Any woman that enhances your money is a keeper.

She and I have a good relationship. She makes me money and I allow her to reap the benefits of having the security and structure she needs. Journi is well educated and cultured. However, she lacks the motivation needed to get herself together. And by get herself together I mean, get a real job or career. Stop fantasizing about dancing and use her brain. I excused her behavior or her lack thereof because she didn't comprehend the need for advancement in life. I blame her upbringing on that. She was content with just making it in life. Somehow, I couldn't bring myself to adjust to just existing in this life. I'm a VP who was trying to get to the CEO level. I need her grind to match my grind. Her status to match my status. Her money to at least get to six digits but not more than that. I don't want a woman that makes more money than me. Women who are the primary bread winners tend to have control issue. I'm the man in the relationship and I plan to keep it that way.

I'll admit falling for Journi was easy. She was breathtakingly beautiful. Her style needed some changing, I made sure she was laced with the best designers and all the name brands she could squeeze into her closet. She fought it at first. However, there was no way I was taking her on trips with me wearing the best fashion that Rainbow has to offer. Journi likes to pretend she doesn't love all the things my money provides for her, but she loves it. She loves the apartment in Midtown, the new BMW I just purchased for her and those zeros in her bank account. I don't love the fact she's with me but still has two feet back in the hood. Going on the trip with her this weekend was out of the question. Her sisters were like her, smart and beautiful and educated. Like Journi, they were hood as hell. Especially her sister Bella, I couldn't stand her. And I don't feel sorry her mom is dead, because I really couldn't stand that bitch. I won't even mention her family. They were the worst. I swear all the family functions ends the same way, in gun fire. I opted to skip that this weekend. Instead I flew down to Miami to get myself a little stress relief. I lied to her about it being work but it doesn't matter. She'll get upset but she always takes me back. I have her hooked on me.

"Bayden, what do you want to eat?"

"Let's go to that little Cuban place."

Lena was moving through our condo with purpose now. She knows I hate being late and when I say let's go, she better be ready. Lena was simple and easy for me. She didn't come close to touching Journi, but she was exactly what I needed. She was something that didn't require me to be everything to her. She wasn't needed or clingy. Too many times I had to validate Journi. She was unsure of herself and needed my approval to take minor steps in the right direction. Lena was the exact opposite. Watching her walk around in a thong and crop top had me ready to bend her over. Her body was proof that Dr. Miami's hands were magic. Lena is a 5'7 cocoa butter goddess, a little short for a model but in today's world height wasn't the first concern. It's mainly about the face and the body. Her tits and ass were both perfect. I met Lena on Instagram. Her pictures were hot. She was trying to break into the industry as a model. I was trying to get some beautiful ladies for a meeting with some clients down in Miami. We made the perfect hook-up. Her purpose and my purpose are the same. We are both motivated by money.

"I think if you keep walking around looking as sexy as you do right now, we may not be going out to eat at all."

"You know compliments will get you everywhere. But not tonight. Meeting with this new agent tonight will get me on the right track to getting more ads and not just on Instagram. I want to look my best and you know if you and I get started my hair will be a mess. You'll just have to wait for all of this soft, wet loving."

Lena bends over with her ass facing me and moves her thong to the side. She lightly sucks her finger removes it from her mouth and sticks it right up her bald sensual plump pussy lips. When she moans, I feel my manhood growing. "Don't tease me baby."

"Don't worry I plan to make sure you're satisfied all night tonight."

I watch her walk toward the steps to go upstairs to get dressed. Tonight, is about business and pleasure. I get to watch Lena work her magic with this agent and I get the pleasure of taking her home and doing all the nasty stuff him and everyone tonight will be thinking about doing to her.

After enjoying our Cuban meal. We head over to the club where Lena was meeting with the agent. I suggested she leave her old agent because the only thing he was doing for her was trying to get her a spot on Love and Hip-Hop Miami. Lena is not a rapper or singer; the show would not have been beneficial to her career. Getting to the club we bypass the line and head straight to the doors. People spot Lena and start screaming her name and taking pictures. She of course puts on a great show by smiling and waving. This is where she sparkles and shines. This is her thing. The dress she's wearing tonight is bright red with a deep cut in the back. There was a long split up the side showcasing her well-toned legs. Her walk through the club was deadly and had me filled with pride. Every woman was looking, and every man was wishing. They could look and wish all they want; she is all mine.

The agent is perfect for the brand Lena and I want for her career. He understands the direction we need to take and how we need to get there. I say we because I believe in Lena's potential. Her booking jobs with high-profile companies leads to me meeting and networking with more high-profile companies. After all she needs to take her management everywhere with her. This is a great working relationship.

"I thought that went great what about you?"

"Oh yeah babe he's perfect for your career. I can already see you now doing everything from hair commercials to walking the runway in Milan."

"I can see it too! I can't wait to get home to thank you."

She was showering me with kisses and her hands were roaming all over my body. I hold her hands together, "slow down baby. There's just one more thing I need for you to do." I place a few soft kisses on her hands. "I have some clients coming through. Call a few of your friends to come through."

"Come on Bayden, haven't we worked enough tonight. I'm exhausted. I just want to go home and enjoy my time with you."

"This is a big deal for me. I need you to be on ready all the time. A big deal for me is a big deal for you."

"I know but—"

"But nothing. You know work is important to me. I thought you said it was important to you too. I just hooked you up with one of the best agents in the country and now that I need you it's fuck me." I could see her thinking, but I didn't have time for the games. I stand to remove myself from her touch.

"I'm sorry. I'll call my girls. Don't be mad at me."

"I'm not mad. I'm building just like you. I need you to see my vision like I see yours." I was spreading it on thick, but I need her to feel it, so she never doubts or questions me. That's Journi's problem she questions me on everything. I need a woman that will just do it. Lena was almost there. I just need to push her more. "I told you my old girlfriend was never supportive of me, don't be her."

"I'm not her. You know that. Give me a minute and I'll have the girls here in no time."

"Thank you, baby." I give her a kiss on the cheek and take out my phone to hit up my clients to let them know to come through tonight. I paid a lot for the VIP section tonight and by all means I plan to use it. Once the clients and her girls get here the party is on. She knows how this will go. My clients will pay top dollar for tonight's entertainment and if the girls are willing, they will pay top dollar for an after party with them. Lena is lucky she no longer has to please my clients. She gets to please me. "Make sure they're beautiful and they bring their A game." If my clients are happy it's more big deals for me. Working my way toward the top was easy. It's staying at the top and going to the next level that's hard. The higher I climb the worst the clients get. They require discretion and had requests that made me cringe. That's really how I meet Lena. I had a client that was obsessed with her. He followed her like crazy on Instagram. He showed me her pictures and I had to admit she was bad. I booked her for his event. Needless to say, he paid a great amount of money to have her in his bed that night. He couldn't stop talking about how great she was in bed. I had to experience it myself. The difference was I didn't have to pay as much as him. Lena in bed was the complete opposite of Journi in bed. She was unbelievable. She had no inhibitions and she never waited for me to take the lead.

Lena is to me what Journi once was. She was open and willing to follow my lead. She was going to elevate my career to the next level. The only difference between her and Journi is Lena had too many miles on her. She's not the girl I'll take home to meet my mom. She's not the girl that can hold a conversation at my company gatherings. That was all Journi. Right now, I need both of them. I can't afford to let either one of them out of my life. I send Journi an ***I miss you text***, then I email my assistant to send her some flowers on tomorrow. She's upset now but she always forgives me. I'm the best thing that's ever happened to her. In the meantime, I watch Lena work the section and I can't wait to get her back to the apartment I got for her. She likes to call it our home. I call it a little break with benefits. And tonight, I'm going to enjoy all the benefits.

Chapter 3

Random Encounters

Journi Fields

Alexa play . . . Drop One Da Producer. . .Bald Head Heaux Shit (feat. KayyPee)

All I can think about is Bayden and how he was my world. Every emotion was running through me. I feel scared and alone. My heart was hurting and there was nothing my sisters could say to me that would cheer me up. They suggested we leave a little earlier for our weekend trip, we hit the road this morning. I hate the ride but the anticipation of seeing family and friends was always worth it. I suggested we just hop on a plain, but my sisters want me to use this time to get myself together. They said I could grieve the relationship but once we hit I-10 I need to throw it out the window.

"Drink one more drink Karman and make us have to stop one more time. I swear, I will pull on the side of the road and let you piss by a bush."

"Bella, your mouth always open. Shut up. I'll drink whatever I want. Here Journi, I got you all your favorite snacks."

Karman tosses me a bag with chips, candy, cookies and drinks. "Thank you boo."

"I told her you weren't going to eat all that mess, but she insisted on getting it."

"Journi, tell her it's comfort food. Who turns down comfort food? Oh, I forgot miss perfect Bella and her perfect figure."

I crack a smile at Karman's remarks. She was absolutely right. Bella's body is perfect. Of the three of us Bella is the most health conscience. She always eats right and exercises. Unlike me and Karman. Bella is 5'8 with chocolate skin that could only be called southern decadence because it glows like the sun came down and kissed her directly. From head to toe she's a perfect size 10. Although, most women that slender don't have a shape Bella has hips, ass and breast that give her a Melissa Ford video vixen look. Karman's body is crazy, she reminds you of Rihanna, except she's a golden goddess that stands at 5'6 with curvy hips and a nice size ass. And then there's me. I'm the youngest but I fall right in between my sisters. I'm 5'7 with mocha brown skin and thick everywhere. Whatever skipped Bella and Karman was given to me in abundance.

I open the bag and every snack I love is in it. I open the dill chips and pickle first and start snacking. "Thank you, Karm, I swear this is the best."

"I don't know about y'all, but I'm excited about everything that's planned for the weekend. Did you get the text from Monica letting us know all she planned?" Bella was smiling too hard.

Karm smiles. "I saw it and I think it's a lot. Let me just say Monica is out of her mind and I'm here for every moment."

Our cousin Monica is turning thirty this weekend. She's having a ***Goddess' Dirty Thirty.*** I have to admit Monica celebrates her life to the fullest. "How do you think she comes up with this stuff?"

"Journi it's Monica. She's been partying and planning party's since we were kids. She was always in the classroom planning someone's birthday party. I swear she was born with it in her blood. Remember the last party her *Flashback to 80's Back*

That Ass up I'm Twenty-five. I was hungover for days and Bella over here was lost for two days."

"I wasn't lost. I was under some dick so good it took me two days to enjoy it, ride it and recover from it."

"Bella!" I swear no filter.

"I'm serious, it was perfect. And he knew how to hit my spot every single time he entered me." She shakes. "It gives me chills just thinking about it."

Karman looks at her. "It gave you more than chills. It gave your ass a court case."

"Oh shit, I forgot about that. He hit your crazy spot." I couldn't believe Bella was locked up behind some dick.

"I can laugh about it now but at the time I wasn't laughing."

"What did you do to land your ass in jail?" Bella never wanted to talk about why we were bailing her ass out of jail in the middle of the night. She said she would tell us one day. Bella let's out a deep sigh and Karman turns the radio down. I pop open another snack like I'm at the movies and it's about to get to the good part.

"After the two days he and I would talk and hook-up. Well the hook-ups turned into spending the weekends together and spending a few days a week together. After a while I felt like we were headed toward a relationship. I decided to drop by his place one day surprise him." She turns and looks at us. "I know, bad idea. But he and I were spending almost every day together. He said he wasn't feeling well, I got him some soup and juice and brought it over to him. When I got there this woman answers the door. And I don't mean ugly woman, she was drop dead gorgeous.

For a minute I thought I had the wrong place. She asks who I'm looking for and I tell her, and she calls him to the door. This fool says he doesn't know me, and I need to leave before I upset his wife."

"Wife!" Karm and I say together.

"You heard me his wife. I dumped that hot soup on his head got out of there but not before fucking up his car. I slashed his tires, busted the windows and his headlights before the police got there."

I fall out laughing, "Bella, you are crazy. What was he doing?"

"He was standing there looking crazy. I told him to come try and stop me and I would bust him up worse than the car."

Karman is sitting there smiling, "Serves his ass right. Why men always feel the need to cheat? Did the wife try to stop you?"

"Nope, she stood there with a smirk on her face. When he kept trying to explain to her that he didn't know me she would put her hands up and tell him this was the last time he makes a fool out of her. I knew then I wasn't the first. But I got him back for both of us."

I look at Karm and we both stare at Bella. "What do you mean got him back for both of *us*? Wasn't the car damage enough?" Bella has a devilish look on her face.

"Cars can be repaired. Egos on the other hand can't. I fucked his wife and we sent him pictures of her, me and another male friend."

"What!" Bella is very open about sex. That decadence in her skin had to have made her very self-indulgent. She doesn't call herself bi-sexual or put labels on what she is. She just enjoys herself.

"Bella you didn't?" Karm is shocked.

"Karm, didn't I say she was gorgeous. I enjoyed it just as much as she did. The kicker is she enjoyed it so much she wouldn't stop calling me. She divorced him and she bats for the other team now."

"Look at my sis turning them out. One woman at a time." I fall out laughing and snapping my fingers. Karm just rolls her eyes.

"You're having fun now Bella, but you will need to pick a side sooner or later. The right man or woman won't want to share you."

"The right man or woman will understand me and my needs. I make it clear up front what I want and what I need. Unlike you I don't run from my desires. I embrace them."

"I'm not running from nothing."

"Big sis, if you don't know what you're running from I won't be the one to tell you."

I don't won't to be the one to tell them they are both running from love. But they are. They run from relationships like it's a disease. They refuse to even let a man get close to them. I'm the only one that craves love and wants it in my life. It gets silent for a minute. "We all running from something. I can already see me running right to the bathroom after all these damn snacks." They burst out laughing.

The reminder of the ride was spent with us laughing and talking about everything under the sun. When we arrive in New Orleans, we check into the Harrah's Casino hotel. All I want to do is take a hot shower and go to sleep but my sisters have different plans. They were ready to hit the club inside the casino. "I really don't want to go." I was trying to give Karm the sad eyes because she would fall for it but Bella steps in front of her.

"Stop playing on Karm's emotions. You know she's soft on you. Not me. You're coming. Remember the rules we set when we got in the car. *You can be sad now but once we got here you had to toss all that sadness away.* Guess what baby girl, we're here and we will have a good time. We're going to party so hard; you'll forget your heart was even broken."

I let them drag me to the club which was crazy. It was good music, good drinks and a good time. We were dancing like our lives depend on it. We sit down to catch our breath and cool down for minute. We were about to wave down a waitress, but she walks over and starts handing us drinks. She told it was compliments of a few admirers. We tell her to thank them and we order another round. A few minutes later two guys walk up and ask my sisters to dance. They didn't want to leave me, but I told them go and have a good time. Besides I need a moment and a little space.

I decide to walk around the casino and play a couple of games. I play a few of the slot machines and end up at the Roulette table. I pick a number and place my bet and I win. I was playing and winning for a good ten minutes before someone whispers in my ear.

"You make winning look easy."

My first reaction was to turn around and check him for getting that close to me. However, it was something about the way he said it or rather the melodic sound of his voice. It was smooth like velvet. Raspy with just a touch of sexiness that wasn't over-whelming and it didn't seem like he was trying to be. His words just, flowed. I decided to let it go and just go with it. Maybe it was all the drinks in me. "It is easy."

"I think you have the magic touch."

"Nope, I'm just picking random numbers."

"It seems strategic to me. I notice you keep betting on black."

"Haven't you heard, always bet on black." He reaches over me, and the scent of his cologne invades my nostrils like aliens taking over a planet. It was slow and steady but with force. He places some chips on the same black five I did. I watch the wheel spin and sure enough it lands on a five, black. I win and so does he. If he was smelling good and sounding good, he was probably ugly. I didn't want to turn around and ruin it.

"Don't worry I always do. Black is beautiful. It's powerful and inspiring. It's sensual with hints of seduction. It's radiant the way it pulls you in with all its curves and beauty. Almost craving and calling me to touch it, to see if its real."

I giggle. Yep it was the drinks. All the shots were kicking in and I was feeling them. His words were sexy, and I must admit they had me curious. I had to turn around to see who was behind the words. I turn and my eyes are met with the most delicious man I've ever seen. I had to look up because he was taller than me, at least 6'5 or 6'6. He wasn't massive in size, but his build was enough to cover me. His skin was like chocolate on top of chocolate. It's smooth like butter and I want to reach out and see if it feels the way it looks. He has the sexiest goat tee that works on him and this low cut Caesar with waves for days. He smirks when my eyes finally meets his. His eyes were gray. They were beautiful and breath taking. I was taken aback by how handsome and good looking this stranger was to me. Before I could say anything, I hear my sisters calling my name.

"Journi, come on we got an invite for a party happening right now. Let's go."

Karm walks up to me grabbing my arm, breaking me away from the stare down I was having with this handsome creature. "A party? What kind of party?"

"Don't worry about it, cash out the chips and let's go. Our ride is waiting."

Bella was signaling for the casino attendant to pass me my winnings. We didn't know anyone to get a ride anywhere. These two right here were about to get us in all kinds of craziness. "Do we even know them?" Bella looks at me and tilts her head.

"We know enough to know we about to have a good time." She sticks her tongue out like Cardi B and starts twerking.

"Listen we will not be out here doing bald headed ho shit." They were acting like we were in college and hopping from party to party with whoever or whomever we were feeling for the night.

Bella starts cracking up. "Yes, we are, come on.

Before I know it, they were pulling me away from the table. I turn around to see the chocolate stranger smiling at me. I have never in my life seen a man so damn handsome and so flawlessly built. I was relieved my sisters was dragging me away. It's men like that, that get you in trouble. Men like that, that make you lose all your senses and all your control. That was something I didn't need in my life. Especially not right now.

Chapter 4

Business and Pleasure

Mecca Adams

Alexa play . . . Tyrese. . . Body Language

"Did you at least get her name?"

"Her friends grabbed her before I got a chance to get it." Aspen, was standing next to me while we watched three beautiful women walk away.

"Some fake ass dudes went over and claimed credit for sending them the drinks. I think they leaving with them. It's probably for the best. That sexy chocolate one had me thinking about proposing marriage."

I knew exactly what Aspen was talking about. I was watching shorty move on the dance floor and everything about her was beautiful. Her smile, the joy in her eyes and her body. Her body had me mesmerized. We ordered them some drinks with the intent of going over to introduce ourselves, but I had an urgent business call that I needed to take. "Damn shame they're gorgeous."

"You never know. It's a small city we could run into them again. Or tomorrow there may even be a better crop of beauties. This city does have some beautiful women."

I agree with Aspen. Each time I travel here I was drawn in by the food, the music and the women. They were naturally beautiful. Aspen and I are from New York and don't get me wrong, the women in New York are exceptionally beautiful as well. It's just something about these down south beauties. I spent a few summers down here and each summer I fell in lust with a different girl. I chuckle to myself just thinking about the beautiful bodies and faces I had the pleasure of having. None of them were like her. A text on my phone alerts me that I need to focus. "We need to go and get this mess taken care of tonight. I got the information we need."

"Is it who we thought it was?"

"It is. I guess she just couldn't help herself. There's nothing more dangerous than a women scorned."

"You got that right. Let's roll. Damn that chocolate one was sexy as fuck. If I run into her again, it's on and popping."

I just shake my head. I force that beautiful beauty to the back of my mind and get my game face ready. Tomorrow is a big day. Tonight, we need to gather all the information, all of our proof so we can present it to the client.

I hate early morning meetings; we scheduled the meeting for noon. We head down a hall which leads to some stairs in the back of the casino. Security checks us out and leads us toward an elevator. Once off the elevator we head toward a meeting room where the client is waiting. We walk into a room with five board members and the president Mr. Coles seated.

"Good afternoon gentlemen. I hope you have some news that will benefit us today."

Mr. Coles looks like he hasn't slept in weeks. He's an antsy short white man that reminds me of kernel Sanders. Complete with white mustache and white eye-brows. Usually his suit completes the look but today he only has on dress slacks and a dress shirt. This is probably his laid back look. "Good afternoon everyone. Please give us a minute to get everything set up." Aspen walks over and turns on the video equipment in the room. He inserts the flash drive, presses some keys to bring up the video and files we have stored on it. "Mr. Coles your security here is extremely tight. Your cameras hear and see everything like all casinos. However, no system is perfect and yours has some flaws. The good thing is we found them all and we can get them plugged up for you. The bad thing is your money may never be recovered."

Aspen and I are owners of a security company. We're the guys a company calls when they've exhausted all the other generic security companies. Our methods are non-traditional and that's what works for us. Hell, we're non-traditional. We don't look like tech geniuses and it works for us. We have the advantage of having street knowledge which helps us to read people and see situations from a different perspective. Someone or should I say a group was robbing this casino blind. They've already gotten away with over six hundred thousand dollars. It would've been less if they would've called us sooner. However, they went through three different security companies before calling us. The other security companies were geeks behind computers who thought all they needed to do was watch the security cameras. We know better. The team working this casino is smart and unconventional. They didn't use slide of hand to steal money or computerized gadgets to make the slot machines drop extra money. They used people. People who work here day in and day out taking home less and less every day. People who have growing families and mounting bills. People who need a quick come up.

We've been in and out this casino working on this case for more than three months. I have to admit they were good. If you blinked to hard you missed everything that was right in front of your face. They all have worked for the casino for years. They knew the inner workings and how to get around everything with no problem. They were an unlikely group consisting of three dealers, one security guard, two cashiers and two janitorial workers. We had proof of how they were stealing and had video of all of them meeting outside of the job. We had bank statements of large deposits and receipts from recent purchases. Enough evidence to get them fired and put behind bars. When we were done Mr. Cole was speechless. He was dumbfounded that undereducated, minimum wage workers could pull off something so seamless and smooth.

Mr. Coles clears his throat, "I don't understand how they were able to get those codes. No one knows those codes."

"No one but you Mr. Coles."

"Yes, I know all the codes and I have access to all the keys. That's casino procedure. I have access to everything in this casino. Me and the general manager in my absence."

Aspen puts a picture up and the general manager immediately recognizes it. He turns beet red. "Aspen you have the floor." This is Aspen's favorite part. He loves giving the gut punches. And I love watching how uncomfortable his ass makes everyone in the room.

"Mr. Coles do you remember Holly Hillsworth?"

"No, I can't say I do. Did she work for the casino?"

"Not only did she work for the casino, but it appears her and your general manager were very intimate. It appears she was his mistress for years. When he ended things with her, she wasn't happy about it. She came up with a plan to rob this casino blind.

We can only assume the codes were discussed at some point in the relationship and the keys and the floor plans were obtained in that relationship as well. Either it was given willingly, or it was taken. I think that's up to Mr. Green to explain."

As each picture of Holly continues to flash on the screen, I can see the embarrassment set in on Mr. Green's face. His old ass got played by a twenty-five year old grad student from Tulane University. There was nothing else for us to say. "We'll leave all of the findings here with you. You have enough here to get a hefty criminal case filed against all the parties involved." Mr. Coles presses a button and security enters the door. He points to Mr. Green and they grab him up out his seat and take him out the door.

"I'll be honest, when my partners in Vegas recommended you guys, I was unsure. When I met you both I was even more hesitant. Today I've learned something my grandmother told me when I was a child. *Don't judge a book by its cover."*

Aspen smirks, "Don't worry we get it all the time. I think it's because Mecca is so ugly. If it wasn't for my good looks and charm, we wouldn't get any jobs."

"You have our information if you need anything from us." We gathered our belongings and walk toward the door. "Mr. Coles you may want to change all the codes and get all the access door keys changed. Everyone have a good day." When the door closes, I push Aspen, "Good looks huh?" Aspen is a walking billboard. He is tattooed from head to toe and even his fingertips. He's charming to no one but the ladies. Aspen and I are both street and hood, but Aspen still wears his hood like a medal of honor. I can at least tuck mine in most days. When Aspen walks into the room dressed like Gucci Mane, the clients usually gasp and the comfort level in the room changes. No one calms down until the moment we resolve the problem. It's fine with us. We actually like it that way. It makes sending that bill to their judgmental asses all the sweeter.

"You know I'm the handsome one. I got brains and good looks."

"I think Mr. Green has a lot of explaining to do."

"They won't let him get nothing out. They'll have him tossed in the swamp before he can say a word."

I nod my head. It's true. We've heard many, many stories about all the bodies out in Vegas. Mr. Coles has the same connections. We know it'll end the same way. "You know they will. Let's hit Bourbon Street and grab some drinks. We need to celebrate this easy ass money." Bourbon was just a short walk away from the casino. This job was complex; however, it wasn't difficult. I believe if you work hard you can play even harder.

We're enjoying ourselves, sitting at the Tropical Isle drinking a few drinks. Out of nowhere I hear a familiar voice. "I know I'm not hearing things."

"Nope I hear it too. I knew he would surface sooner or later."

I turn around and scan the bar. I spot him. "Legend, what are you doing here?" I dap him up. Way before me and Aspen went to school and became businessmen we ran wild in the streets of New York. We got caught and served some time in juvie. That's when we met Legend. He was only a bit older, but he had been in the streets his entire life. He took us under his wing and taught us everything we needed to know. When we got out no one could touch us on the streets. We started making fast money. I was able to take care of my mom and Aspen was able to take care of his family. Business was good until I was shot three times. After that I took my money and went to school. Aspen decided to go with me.

But not Legend. He said the streets called his name and he needed to answer. The last time I'd seen Legend was about three years ago. At that time, he was attempting to transition his illegal business into a legal business. We gladly set up his security system and gave him our best security packages. We showed him how to wash his money and make it all look legal. For everything we taught him he wanted to pay us, but Legend is family you don't charge family. Once the set up was done business started to pick up and we've been moving from state to state for a few years. We haven't been home to New York in three years.

"Oh shit, if you two are in town that means one thing it's double trouble time. And now that we're all together it's about to be the triple threat all over again. What the hell are you guys doing down here?"

"We had a job."

"Always about your money. I can respect that about you two but hey let me buy you guys another round. We can get it to go."

Two hours later we all were hanging out on a balcony overlooking everyone and laughing about old times. We find out Legend came down with Swiss, another guy we knew from back home. They were down taking care of business. We didn't ask what kind of business and Legend didn't offer that information. I was scanning the street watching the crowds passing through. When a group of women walking by catch my eye. I can't believe it's her. I watch her walk into the bar across from us. I tap Aspen to let him know I'll be back in a minute. I walk into the bar which isn't crowded, I see the group of ladies. I notice they all have on the same shirt. One of them walks pass me and I read the front, *The Goddess' Dirty Thirty*, on the back is a name. I stand back and watch shorty for a minute. She is beautiful. I notice she's with the same ladies she was with last night. They look like they are related. I watch as shorty attempts to flag down one of the shot girls. When she turns her back, I read the back of her shirt, *Mocha Goddess*. It describes her perfectly. Her skin is flawless I can tell even through the light make-up she has on. When the crowd turns their attention to the middle of the floor, I notice a bull. While the attention is on the bull, I slide behind her, "We have got to stop meeting like this Miss Mocha Goddess." She turns and smiles at me. Even her smile is beautiful.

"Mocha Goddess huh? I like that."

She licks her lips. It's a simple act that's filled with seduction. "It's on the back of your shirt." I smile when she looks down at her shirt.

"I forget how strong these drinks are down here."

I extend my hand, "I'm Mecca. And you are?"

She twirls around, "The Mocha Goddess, but you can call me Journi."

"Are you enjoying the party with your friends?"

"Those are my sisters, Bella and Karman. The party is not until later tonight. This is a just the double dare scavenger hunt."

I was confused, "A what?"

"You know, *I double dare you*."

I get so close to her I can smell the shots on her breath and the sweet fragrance she's wearing, "You double dare me to do what?" Before she could answer the music in the bar stops and someone comes on the mic.

"I double dare two people to ride the bull together and stay on for more than two minutes. The prize is an extra 50 points."

I look around the bar and the ladies were lined up ready to go. This was about to be good to watch. Each one falls down. Journi's sister Bella walks over. She looks me up and down and then she looks at Journi.

"Who's your friend?"

"Bella this is Mecca."

She shakes my hand. "Nice to meet you." She turns back to Journi, while I text Aspen to come on over.

"You ready sis?"

"Ready for what?"

"To ride that bull. And don't be trying to act cute for your friend over here. Matter of fact show him those skills of yours. Let's go I double dare your ass!"

Journi looks at me and smiles. "Well you've been dared. Are you going to chicken out?" She licks her lips again.

"I thought I told you last night always bet on black."

Her and her sister head to the middle of the floor where the bull is and the first one to hop on is Journi. She didn't even use the step she just jumps right on up there and positioned that round ass up in glorious view that would make grown men cry. I peep her sister Bella standing on the side just watching. The bull is moving in slow motion, its hypnotizing to watch her work her body on that bull. Those hips, that ass, her smile all working overtime. Out of nowhere I see Bella approaching. I was wondering what she was about to do when the bull dips down low trying to knock shorty off, she hops right on the back of the bull behind Journi. Both of them ride that bull like they were being paid money to do it. The show they are putting on has everyone cheering and in a trance. I enjoy a woman who can relax and allow herself to have fun. A woman that offers just the right amount of sex appeal without crossing the line of seeming easy and accessible to every man. There was something about her body language. Journi has this innocence that floats around her, but her eyes and actions read bad girl. I like good girls, they ground me. Bad girls please me but they are not keepers. The combination of both has me curious. I look over my shoulder and see Aspen with Legend and Swiss in tow. Aspen walks over and whistles.

"That's a beautiful site right there."

"Man, who you telling."

Legends taps me on the back. "This is why I love this city. Let me get them a round they'll need it after that ride."

"I already got it. I got the whole party a round." I wink at the shot girls heading over to the group of ladies that are surrounding Journi and Bella giving them hi-fives and hugging them. I see the confused look on everyone's face. "It's a birthday party. The one with the crown on her head is turning thirty. The three ladies are sisters."

"Sisters huh? They all fine, but that dark chocolate is mine."

"That's Bella." I let Aspen know. Journi was headed back over by me when Swiss grabs her arm. Giving no thought at all I turn toward him when I feel Aspen's hand on my shoulder. Journi looks him up and down and eyes me. Swiss gets the hint.

"Damn shorty my bad. I just wanted to holla at you for a minute."

I grab her hand and pull her close to me. "She's good Swiss."

"Damn Mecca, you hating as usual."

I didn't want to take Swiss's comments as disrespect, I just pass it off as him being drunk. Journi stands in front of me and smiles. "That was quite a show."

"I was just checking off this list. My cousin said thank you for the drinks." Journi waves her sisters over. "You met Bell. This is Karman my other sister."

"Nice to meet you Karman. This is Aspen, Legend and Swiss." I see the birthday girl heading our way. "Happy birthday beautiful!" I swear this family must have a gorgeous gene in their line because they are all beautiful. Journi looks at me and all four of them reach down in the bags they are carrying.

"My cousin's birthday party is tonight we want to invite you guys. It's a special private party. You can come if you promise to follow all the rules."

I look Journi dead in her eyes. "I'm not great with rules." She doesn't break eye contact with me.

"See and I was hoping to see you again. Oh well. Nice meeting you guys."

Aspen stops them, "Hold up ladies he doesn't speak for all of us. I'm good at rules." He gives them a schoolboy smile while undressing Bella with his eyes. She walks over to him.

"I know you lying. You look like you'll break all the rules. Don't mind Journi, she's a teacher she likes rules. Not me and not tonight. Tonight, I feel like doing something that will get me expelled."

We all start laughing because Aspen is speechless. They hand us a brown envelope and turn to walk away. I open my envelope and in it is an invite for the party and a mask. "What the hell is a Face Covered, Ass Out Party?" Aspen asks.

"It's one of those lingerie parties. Look at the back it says pajamas and lingerie only. We in for a wild night with these ladies." Just the thought of seeing Journi in something see through had me thinking all kinds of thoughts. And all of them were naughty. Maybe if I'm on my worst behavior she'll punish me.

Chapter 5

I Just Want to Feel Something

Journi Fields

Alexa play . . . Jhene Aiko. . . Happiness Over Everything (H.O.E.)

Sitting on the back of the party bus on the way back to the hotel, I was deep in thought. Karman slides in the seat next to me, "You good sis?"

"I came over here to check on you not the other way around."

Karman is the oldest and she makes sure she takes care of us. "I'm feeling these drinks I know that."

"You back here deep in thought."

"Just thinking about—"

"Please don't say Bayden."

"I wasn't."

"You better not be. Not when you have that fine ass man trying to get with you."

"He is fine as hell and smells so damn good." I swear I love a man that smells like heaven and that's exactly what he smells like. I don't know what he was wearing but whatever it is just works for him. At the casino last night, I wasn't able to get a good look at him but today I got an eye full of his body. He's not basketball player slim but not thick like a football player. He's a good balance right in the middle. Fit and tone and cut in all the right areas. Even fully dressed I could tell. His skin, so dark, so smooth, like black silk. When he smiles, I feel something I haven't felt in years. I feel a longing to be touched. The way he looked at me, had me feeling sexy all over. "It's just a weekend."

"Are you trying to convince me or yourself? Journi, have fun. You don't let yourself do that anymore. I know you. You overthink everything. Don't do that right now. Just go with it but don't let Bella pull you down a rabbit hole if you can't handle it. Know your limits. She has none."

I know what Karm is saying but she was wrong. It wasn't Bella pulling me down a rabbit hole. It was me jumping. For so long I've felt like I was trapped in a box. For years I've been told to act appropriately. To behave like a lady. Don't dress like this, don't talk like that. Today I got to do something that just felt right. I got to be free. To be myself. I got on that bull and had the time of my life. When I was up there riding, I got a glimpse of Mecca watching me. His eyes were judgement free. I wasn't about to look too deep into anything. I just want to enjoy the moment. "And what about you Karm?"

"What about me?"

"Are you coming down the rabbit hole with us?" Karm is all work and no play. It works for her. She's one of the top commercial real estate agents in her firm. Breaking into real estate was easy for her. She's a natural at selling and even better at learning something no one wants her to learn. Commercial real estate isn't easy for a black women to get into because it's a white boys club. But Karm got in there and learned everything, made great connections and knocked down all types of doors for herself. She's focused right now on becoming a broker and owning her own real estate firm. She's ready for that CEO, boss status. I'm proud of her. She's just one of those people that goes to bed with her career instead of a man. "When is the last time you just had fun?"

"It's been awhile. I'm not like you or Bella. It's hard for me to just be free. I mean when we come home like this it's ok but it's because we're among family and friends. Back in Atlanta, I can't just be out there all carefree. My reputation is on the line in everything I do. Image is everything to me."

"True but tonight, put that mask on and let yourself go just a little. At least enough to knock the cobwebs off that thing." Karm looks at me all surprised, but she knows it's true. "Maybe that Legend or Swiss can give you a session good enough to last you for another couple of years."

"It hasn't been years. Only a year."

"Yep that's what I mean you need it. Let's just both not over think tonight. Let's just have fun."

****

"Who let Bella pick out these outfits?" Looking in the mirror I was pissed off I let Bella pick out my outfit. I knew she would pick something crazy but something this revealing. I had on a purple lace booty shorts bustier jumper thing. The bustier is strapless and the lace is so sheer you can see my nipples and it barely covers all my essential parts. My cheeks are hanging out the bottom and if I hadn't gotten waxed my hair would be hanging out the sides. This is way too much, even for Bella. "I can't wear this all night."

"At least you don't have on a damn thong! Bella, I could kill your ass. I swear you do too damn much."

Karm, has on a pink baby doll lingerie set that's shear and see through. When she turns around, she was right, it was a thong.

"Bella! Get out here." Bella walks out the bathroom wearing a black see through two piece lingerie set. The top is V-neck that's super low. Low enough, Bella's boobs was about to pop out and poke us in the eye. The shorts were like mine, see through and showing all her cheeks.

"Oh, y'all look so good."

Karm and I just stare at her.

"Stop tripping. It's a masked, lingerie party. Everyone will be dressed like us. They just won't look as good as us."

"I could choke your ass. You are so damn crazy." There was a knock at the door. Karm opens it and Monique comes in dressed in a silver fishnet type lingerie set. She was looking like an extra for P-Valley.

"Bella, I love this outfit. Thank you so much. I can't wait to get in there and drop it like it's hot."

"Well at least someone likes my style. These heifers in her complaining. I made them look good. Let's go birthday girl. Let's get this party started."

The party was being held at some big mansion off of St. Charles Ave. I have to admit Monique knows how to party. Everything was decorated like we were attending a masquerade ball, but it was a freaky ball. Each area of the house has a different set up with a game. Karm saw a room with a pool table, she was on it. The men are going to be busy watching her ass and she'll be busy collecting cash. Bella saw a room with pole dancing, she wanted me to join her, but I saw a spades game going on and I wanted in on it.

I was standing watching the game going on, waiting on it to end. I swear this outfit I have on is saying open season because every man that has walked past me is staring. I'm a little self-conscience. For the past year Bayden has made comments on how much weight I've gained. I look down at my legs and I wish I would have put on some fishnet stockings or any kind of stockings to hold in everything that was shaking. The game ends and I walk over to take a seat. I can feel eyes on me. I sit down and out the corner of my eyes I see this perfect specimen of a man walking towards the table. I was wrong, maybe he does play football or basketball, his chest is rock solid. He has on a mask, but I know it's him. I can tell by the bottom half of his face, the way his hair is cut low and the mean mug he's wearing. He walks over and takes the seat across from me. I wonder how long he's been in the room. Two other people join us. I can feel him staring at every part of my body. I can't cover up instead I cross my legs. We start and the game goes quick. He's good at signaling me with his eyes. Or maybe I'm just good at reading them. By the third round he and I were taking each couple that sat at our table down. "After this game I need a break."

"Whatever you want beautiful."

It was the way he said it that had my pussy jumping. It was intense yet relaxing. Possessive but endearing. I want him to say more. I want that bass in his voice to continue to vibrate me. To continue waking up a part of me I thought was dead. The game ends and we win again. I get up to stretch my legs. I know he's behind me. There's no need to put an extra bounce in my step because the way these booty shorts are fitting my ass, it's untamed and bouncing all on its own. I stop at the bar and grab a drink. "You play spades really good."

"I had a good partner."

"Are you enjoying the party?"

"I'm enjoying being around you."

"That was bold."

"What's bold is you. I can't take my eye off of you."

He gets close to me, takes his hand and moves the hair from in front my face. My whole body heats up. Someone bumps me from behind and I fall right into his arms. He smells so good I dawdle for a minute. "I'm sorry, someone bumped me." He takes my hand and guides me to another room in the house. This room is only lit up by LED and neon lights. I can hear my song Dance for You playing. I find a chair and motion for him to take a seat. I start dancing for him. I do a slow seductive dance feeling every beat and all the words of the song. With every turn and every dip, I was moving my hips to the beat like a professional. I turn my back to him and touch my toes making sure to bounce each cheek of my ass separately. I ease down into his lap and start grinding on him. I lean back, resting my head on his shoulder and his hand goes to my waist, the other hand is gently around my neck. He licks my neck and nibbles on my ear.

He whispers. "Let me have you."

My only reply is a moan. He taps me to get up and I follow his lead when he takes my hand. We enter a bathroom together. I back up to the wall while he locks the door. Every movement he makes is sexy to me. I've never felt this much attraction to a man. It's overpowering and addictive at the same time. He turns around, our eyes meet. That mean mug he wears is gone, it's replaced with a smile and a softness I hadn't seen before. He walks over to me and takes his finger and traces the outline of my bustier. His fingers move to my nipples and he circles around them. In response they harden, and I can feel the lace between my legs getting wetter and wetter. I attempt to move, I can't he has me pinned against the wall. His hands slide down to my hands and he pulls them up over my head. He pulls a towel from the rack and ties my hands. His fingers don't go back to my nipples but instead he brings them up to my face. He looks excited like a kid in a candy store not knowing what to touch first. His touch is soft and sensual. He parts my lips and kisses me. His lips are soft, I can taste the crown on his tongue. I want more of it, I take my time sucking on his tongue and then his lips. I haven't been kissed like this in a long time. The kiss deepens and I feel him grabbing at the zipper on my outfit. He breaks the kiss and pulls my clothes down. When he gets to my hips, I have to wiggle for him to get it down. He goes slower and stops at piece of lace fabric that's caught in my lips. I open my legs to make it easier for him and he stoops down. I feel his tongue on my belly button, sending instant heat through me. His tongue moves from my belly button all the way down to my lips. He uses his teeth to pull the fabric and takes his tongue moving it slowly and intensely parting my lips. I moan his name, "Mecca."

"I knew you would taste good."

He stops and continues to pull my clothes down. I lift my legs to help him take it off. While my leg is lifted, he takes it and puts it over his shoulder.

"Journi, I asked you a question. You didn't give me and answer."

Before I could respond his tongue was back going down the same path. This time it was going back and forth working my clit. I don't even know what he asked me. I don't remember a question. I couldn't think. When he starts sucking my clit, I wrap my other leg around his neck. Every lick, suck and slurp was pulling an orgasm out of me. I've never had an orgasm just off oral. He's not even using his fingers. Just his mouth is working. But this wasn't average oral, it was an assault on my pussy. I look down because I couldn't believe what was happening to me. When his eyes meet mine a wave so intense hits me, I close my eyes to ride it. The pleasure is freeing and exhilarating. It's euphoric. He removes my legs from around his neck, I struggle to gain my composure. He looks at me and backs up. My hands are still tied so I can't cover my body. I swarm a little under his intense gaze. His body is beyond amazing. His chest is covered with tattoos and I want to lick every one of them. Hell, I just want to lick him to see if he tastes like chocolate. He drops his pajama bottoms; I can see his dick begging to be freed. I walk over to him, lean in and place soft kisses on his neck. I back up and look at the towel that's wrapped around my wrist. It's preventing me from pulling his boxers down. I need to see it. I want to wrap my hands around it. Fuck that, I want to taste it so bad I'm drooling. "Untie me, I want to touch you." I drop my eyes to the monster jumping at the sound of my voice.

"Not yet."

I suck my teeth. "You like this control."

"Nah, shorty, I love control. I'll ask you again, can I, have you?"

He can have all of me. I just wasn't about to say it to him. I want to play, just like he's playing. I stand in front of him biting the side of my lip like I'm thinking. "Make me want it." He smiles and even his teeth are perfect. In one swift motion, again he walks back over to me and turns me around. My face presses against the wall and his hand is around my neck. It's pressure and pain all at the same time. His other hand smacks my ass. It's some kind of 50 shades of grey mess, I've never been into. But this, this passion, this feeling, this intensity is different. I'm enjoying it.

"Don't be naughty. Say it."

I feel his dick on my back, rock hard. When he runs his hands up and down my leg, I quiver from the feeling. When he parts my legs, he slaps his dick against my thigh, I almost cum on myself. I won't let him win. I don't say a thing. His fingers are at my opening, his hold on my neck increases and I can feel the tip of his dick on my ass pressing, waiting for my ok. I don't say a word. Sweat drips down my face. He licks it and my pussy jumps, almost screaming yes for me. Still I don't say a word. The movement of his fingers increases, playing in the stickiness of my opening. When he pinches my clit, I moan.

"I see you play to win. I do too!"

His fingers speed up and I am breathless. His hand is still gripping my neck, his thumb is moving up and down like his fingers in me. How is he able to multi-task like this? My moaning increases and I can't hold it. I'm feeling this intense feeling in my body. It's taking a hold of me. I'm about to cum. I feel his breathe on my skin making the hairs on the back my neck stand at attention.

"Say it Journi. Say it." He removes his fingers and smacks my ass again.

I can't hold it. I cum just from the sound of his voice. "You can have me." The words leave my mouth in between moans.

"Hold on to that window seal."

I do exactly what he says, I feel him smack my ass again and then he lifts me. I swear he's holding me like I'm a light weight. I feel his dick at my opening. I stretch my legs, almost like a split and arch my back. I want the dick. I welcome the dick. I need the dick. When he enters me, he's bigger than I expected. Every inch he jams into me feels like a mixture of pain and pleasure. "Oh Mecca!"

"You say that shit so sexy. Say it again."

I shake my head no. He pulls out and slams back into me over and over. I was trying to hold it again. He releases my legs and turns me around.

"Keep playing with me."

This man was killing my insides and he wasn't even breathing hard or breaking a sweat. He starts kissing me again and makes his way back down to my breast. Everything he was doing was slow and passionate. I want him inside me again. Not being able to touch him was killing me. When he bites my nipple and twirls it around in his mouth, I scream his name, "Mecca!"

"Good girl, you can have this dick again."

I throw my leg over his shoulder. Being dancer has its advantages. I feel like a dog in heat, needing it. When he enters me again, he places soft kisses on my ankle that's over his shoulder and runs his hand up and down my leg. Every touch, every slam, has my juices flowing like the Mississippi river. I've lost count as to how many times I've cum. His breathing increases and he moans my name, I know he's cumming too. I'm spent. I can't move. He releases my leg and then the towel from around my wrist. He kisses each wrist and kisses me again. I watch him walk over to the toilet and flush the condom.

"You're flexible, I like that. I'm not done with you yet. I'm thirsty, let's get a drink."

As I'm wiping myself down, my cheeks burn from me smiling. I can't stop smiling. He's still touching me. It's gentle touches, caressing my cheek, kissing my neck, smelling my hair. This moment should be considered cheap and random, except he wasn't making me feel that way. When we step out and order our drinks, he's standing so close to me I can feel his heartbeat and smell me on his lips. Out of nowhere I can hear fussing and gunshots. He grabs my hand and waist and rushes me out the house. “Wait, I have to get my sisters.”

“They’ll be ok, they’re with my friends. I want to make sure you’re safe. Come on my car is over here.”

Everyone is running and screaming. I don’t want to go without them. He rushes me to the car, I refuse to get in. “Please, I can’t leave without my sisters.” I see someone run pass us covered in blood.

“Journi, get in the car and I promise I’ll call them.”

I agree when I hear more shots. I say a prayer that they are safe.

Chapter 6

Mesmerized

Aspen Carter

Alexa play . . . Tank . . . Dirty

Everything at the party was popping off good. Five minutes ago, Bella and her friend was giving me a lap dance. Maybe I should say Bella was doing most of the dancing. Her friend was enjoying feeling her up. I was enjoying the dance and the show. When I walked into the room tonight Bella was swinging around the pole like she was working at the KOD instead of just enjoying a house party. Every eye in the room was on her and why not? She's the epitome of a sexy walking, talking felony. I sat back and watched her work. When she pulled her friend up and started dancing with her, I figured maybe she was batting for the other team. That was until she made eye contact with me. Through the mask I could see her eyes speaking to me. She was drawn to me and, I damn sure was drawn to her. She pointed my way and they both walked over to me. After the dance I went to grab the ladies a few drinks. When I stepped in the hallway, I notice Swiss standing down the other hallway pacing. Maybe he was waiting on somebody. He looks up and sees me and walks the opposite way. I swear he's been strange since the first day I meet his ass. I see Mecca and Bella's sister come out of a room down the same hallway he was pacing, fixing their clothes and smiling. I knew what they were doing. Waiting on the drinks I hear some fussing followed by shots. I rush to get back to the room with Bella. I grab her and she grabs her friend's hand. I know I need to get them out safely. I knew

Mecca had her sister and I saw Legend with her other sister. I get them to my car.

"Where to ladies?" I was smiling hoping they would be down for whatever.

"Nowhere until I know my sisters are safe."

"I saw them with my crew they good."

"You just trying to get some."

She was right. But I was telling the truth. "Well I planned on getting me more than some. I want all of it." I look at Bella who looks like she's about to hop out of the car at any moment. "Wait I'll prove it to you." I grab my phone to call Mecca. The Bluetooth was ringing in the car because I want to put Bella at ease.

"You good Aspen?"

"You know it. Shit got wild fast—"

"Cut all the damn chit chat, is my sister with you?" Bella interrupted me and all I could do was smile. She was even sexier when she was feisty.

"Bella, I'm good. Is Karm with you?"

"No, I was hoping she was with you. I'm glad you're safe."

"Alright, Mecca, I'll call Legend to make sure he has their other sister cause this one in here is a little feisty, she might fight me. She just don't know I like feisty."

"Simmer down or you won't get no taste of this. I'll text you Journi."

I call Legend next. When he picks up, I can hear him running. "You good man or do I need to roll back around?"

"We good. Just getting to the car."

"Do you have my sister with you?" Bella cuts right to it.

"I got her she's good."

"Nah, let me hear her say it. Put her on the phone."

"My boy wouldn't do nothing to her."

"Still, let me hear her say it."

"Bella, are you safe? Is Journi with you?"

"No, she's with Mecca and I'm with Aspen. I'm glad you're safe. I don't know why Monique's celebrations end in gun fire every year. It's like fire works for her."

"Well, I know why."

It was something about the way her sister said it that had me thinking maybe Legend was behind it. He's always been wild and uncontrollable. "You want me to take you to your sister?" I look over at Bella who shakes her head.

"Karm, I'll text Journi, but you do the same."

"Ok, Bella you coming back to the hotel, right?"

"I wasn't planning on it. You sure you're good?"

"Umm yeah. He's a little touched, you know what I mean."

"Aww baby girl. You can say it out loud. I'm bat shit crazy but I don't play about nobody putting hands on what's mine."

I start cracking up at Legend. He was beyond crazy.

"I'm not yours. You ain't got to defend me."

Bella starts laughing too. "I see you're in good hands Karm. Let that man defend you and get your ass right tonight."

"Yeah, baby girl, let me get you right."

"Bella, I'm going to kill you!"

"See you in the morning Karm."

Bella pushes the end call button and final sits back to relax. "You ladies need a drink before we get in for the night?" I was trying to make sure the mood wasn't ruined. I watch them look at each other for a minute. I want to ask if they know each other. But I don't want to ruin it. I just keep my mouth shut.

Bella turns to me. "We're good. I just want your dick in my mouth and her mouth on this pussy. That's all."

My dick was at attention all over again. I love a woman that doesn't have sexual limitations. Not to mention one that knows how to fully express herself. All that shy shit is for the birds. We're grown, act like it. The birthday party was done but the after party was just beginning. I can tell this was going to be a night to remember.

****

My eyes open to the sound of my phone going off and someone in the shower. I look over and the bed is empty. I grab my phone and check the text from Mecca telling me to meet for breakfast. I sit up in the bed and the bathroom door opens. Bella walks out wrapped in a towel.

"Good morning, soldier."

"Soldier?"

"You were at attention all damn night. I like that in a man."

"Believe me, it was easy to stay at attention just looking at that scrumptious chocolate." It was true. Bella is gorgeous, she's the perfect shape and the perfect size. She drops her towel and I'm at attention all over again. "How about another round before breakfast?"

"My friend already left. It's just me now."

"That's just fine with me. I want you all to myself anyway." I enjoyed every part of last night. I'm usually not a selfish man but I'll admit I was hogging Bella last night. I was enjoying everything about her. She's sensual in a way that I've never experienced in a woman. She's confident about herself and her body. She made sex what it should be...pleasure.

"How about I take a raincheck, I'm starving. And if I know my sisters they are too!"

I get up and let the sheet fall displaying my hard dick. I watch as she licks her lips and smiles, "Let me hop in the shower."

"Yeah, you do that before I change my damn mind."

We arrive at breakfast, I dap up Mecca, Legend and nod to Swiss. I speak to Bella's sisters. The one with Legend is sitting with her arms crossed. We take our seats to order. I look over at Mecca and he's all smiles. He only smiles like that when we wrap up a job. Ole girl must have put it on him last night. I look over at Legend and he's smiling too but his ass always smiling. The look on Swiss' face is unreadable. He doesn't look happy. I wonder if he hooked up with anybody last night. "This is your city beautiful what's good here?"

"I like the French toast. I think it's good here. This place is pretty new, but we've heard good things about it. You look like a steak kind of guy, maybe an omelette for you."

I lean over and whisper in her ear, "I'm more of a seafood guy but I think you know that already."

Legend looks at his date. “I thought you said you lived in Atlanta? I didn’t think you were from the city.”

“I said we live in Atlanta now. I didn’t tell you where I was from.”

“I got you, you just want me to know where I can find you.”

“Who says I want to see you again?”

“Baby, I’m Legend. Everyone wants to see me over again.”

“They must be sad and desperate to want to see a fool like you again.”

We all start laughing because Legend is a true clown. He starts putting his hands on his chest like he’s shocked. She even cracks a smile.

“Look at that Journi, I think Karman may have found her match.”

“Do you all live in Atlanta?” Mecca’s question was for everyone, but his eyes were on Journi.

Bella and Karman look at each other and smile. “I guess you weren’t talking with those lips of yours huh Journi. Maybe, you were just talking with the other set.”

Journi turns red and throws her fork at Bella. These ladies were not only fine, but they’re funny too! Through our conversation at the table I learned Bella is a nurse. I can see her walking around in those tight ass scrubs tempting all her patients. I wanted a little more time with her to get to know her a little better. That wasn’t going to happen they were hitting the road this afternoon. We exchange numbers, to keep in touch. I let her know we have a job coming up in a few weeks out there. I want to hook up again with her. When they exit the restaurant, we sit at the table for a minute.

"I like that girl. What the New Orleans people say? That redbone Karman. She's smart and fine." Legend was licking his lips and clapping his hands together like he was Birdman.

"I like Bella too. She's wild as fuck but I like that shit. When is the job in Atlanta coming up?" I look over at Mecca who pulls out his phone.

"It's next month but we need to get out there a little sooner."

"I might hit up Atlanta with you. I got to see that redbone thing again."

"Man, Legend she wasn't even talking to you. She was over your ass. What the hell did you do to her?" Karman wasn't feeling him at all. She wasn't even talking to his ass.

"Check this out right. Last night, we chilling at the party. I get up to go to the bathroom. Come back and some fool smiling in her face. She's not feeling him, I can tell because I know she into me. I tell his ass move the fuck on. He gets upset, talking about I'm blocking and shit. We going back and forth and shit. She was like, *Legend, it's cool come on let's get a drink*. This fool grabs her arms and she slaps him. Then, I punched him. He pulls out his gun like I'm scared. You know what I say."

We all answer, "Don't pull it out, unless you plan to use it!"

He starts smiling hard as hard. "See, I taught you well. I took that shit out his hand and beat him with it. His boys came in, we start fighting and they start blasting. You know me and Swiss was ready."

I just shake my head. I knew it was him. "I knew that was your ass. I knew when Bella called her sister last night and she was mad."

"Yeah, she was mad but check this, she was helping me fight when his boys popped up. I like my chicks with a little hood in them."

Mecca looks at him. "Legend you just like chicks."

"Yeah, that's true. It's been good catching up but me and Swiss got some business to handle. Hit me up before you roll out of town. As usual hooking up with you two led to a legendary night of wild fun. I enjoyed myself. Maybe next time Swiss will too."

"Bruh, all them fine women in there last night and you didn't hook up with any of them?" I look at Swiss who starts mean mugging Mecca. But Mecca doesn't even notice because he's cracking up.

"Don't worry about me. I just didn't get the one I wanted. But everything comes in time." He looks Mecca up and down and walks away and Legend was out right behind him.

"Damn, Mecca I think he wanted Journi."

"He salty as hell about it too! He always been a nigga that wants what someone else got. I got her already. She's good."

"I thought he would've grown out of it. If you ask me, I think he always wanted what you had."

"Some people just don't change at all."

I was trying to think of a way to break the news to Mecca. I didn't want to ruin his good mood. He's been trying to keep our hands clean but sometimes we need to get them a little dirty. "Before we leave, I got a call from the Casino."

"I'm not surprised. I figure they would call. They need us to clean up their mess."

"They want it kept quiet and in house. I got a feeling if they contact the bosses in Vegas it's going to be a lot more heads rolling."

"It'll cost them."

Lately Mecca has been on this straight and narrow track. He likes being completely legal. I like getting my hands dirty. I think the dirty humbles you and keeps you hungry. I never want to forget what hunger felt like. What broke felt like. The smell of blood and fear reminds me of it. It motivates me. "They agreed to pay double our fee. I can turn them down. But you know it's been a minute."

"Go ahead and accept it. Beside if I don't let this out, I might take it out on Swiss."

I was glad he was on board. The jobs go smoother with him. Plus, he knows he needs it, just like me. "I'll let them know. I'll be honest. I'm looking forward to that job in Atlanta. I like that Bella."

"Yeah, I like Journi. You like Bella that much? You're usually not a repeat offender."

He was right. I'm a one and done type of guy. "There's just something about her." If I get to have her one more time maybe, she'll be out of my system.

Chapter 7

An Afterthought

Journi

Alexa play . . . SWV. . . You're Always on My Mind

Getting ready to go on my second interview had my nerves on edge. I'm excited about the position at a local high school. If I get the job not only would I get to teach but I'll get the opportunity to become the coach for the dance team. It's my dream job. Maybe not the dream school but I can make it work. My phone dings, I smile. I know it's not him this morning but for some reason, Mecca still runs across my mind. He and I have talked daily since meeting two weeks ago. He was surprisingly a much needed breathe of fresh air to me. The things he and I did the first night still makes me blush. When he told me, he would call me after breakfast that morning, I didn't believe him. I took what we did as a one-night stand. I expected to never hear from him again. When he called, I was shocked and excited all at the same time. The things this man did to my body. It was like we were lovers in a past lifetime. Our conversations are endless some days which helps me. Since most of my free time is spent with him, I don't have time to think about Bayden. A man who hasn't tried to contact me or call me. It's like I meant nothing to him. I wasn't planning on taking him back, but I at least want to know I meant something to him.

I hear the downstairs doorbell ring. I rush down to answer it. When I open the door it's a delivery guy with three boxes of beautiful white roses. I grab them and read the card. ***Your smile***

alone will wow them today. You got this, Beautiful! They're from Mecca he's the only person I know that calls me *beautiful.*

I start smiling, it's something about him. This man's attention to detail was outstanding. He told me he wouldn't call this morning because he had business to handle, I wasn't expecting this at all.

"Who was at the door?" Bella comes down the stairs dressed and ready for her shift at work.

I've been staying with her and Karman. "It wasn't for you; it was for me." I fling around showing off my flowers. Not a minute later Karman comes down the stairs.

"Who was at the door?"

"It wasn't for us Karm. It was for the pussy fairy over here. She done sprinkled that pussy juice so good he sending her flowers and shit."

I turn around and hit her arm, "Jealous much?"

"Journi, you must have whipped it on him good. Teach Bella, her sprinkles don't work no more."

"Fuck you Karm. I wasn't trying to whip nobody. I was having fun."

"I wasn't trying to whip nobody. I was having fun too! He was just an amazing lover." I turn around and they're both staring at me.

Bella snaps her fingers, "Details, details, details!"

"Nope, no details. He just made my body feel amazing. Every touch, every stroke sent chills through my body. I've never had orgasms like that. It was like his dick was having a conversation with my pussy." Karman looks at me.

"Oh, what were they saying to each other?"

"Everything and nothing and too much all at the same time." Bella almost flips out her seat.

"He was hitting that spot. Bang, bang, bang!"

"Bella, your ass is crazy. He hit all the spots. Spots I never even knew I had. He had that hook and it had me shook!" We hi-fived each other and start laughing.

"Now Journi, don't open another door before you close the other one."

"Damn Karm, you can ruin a wet dream. Let me go while I'm still imagining a hook in me hitting them spots. Carry on Reverend Karm."

Bella walks out and Karm walks over to me. "I'm not trying to preach. I think it's good you like Mecca and he likes you. I'm just saying don't open the door when you still have another foot in the other door."

"I'm not opening any doors. I'm just having fun."

"I'm just saying you are barely over Bayden and you're already on to the next man."

"He and I are just talking. Damn Karm!"

"Again, I'm not preaching. I'm just saying baby girl."

"You are preaching! Believe me, I would know if I was opening doors."

"How would you know you're opening doors? You don't even know you was making love."

Karman walks out the room and out the door before I could say another word. I wasn't opening doors and Mecca and I wasn't making love. Were we? You can't make love to someone without being in love with them. We don't even know each other like that. Karm is always preaching. Just because she's the oldest she thinks she knows it all. She thinks she's slick. She's the one opening doors. I know her ass been in contact with Legend. I take another look at the roses and walk out the door to head over to my interview. As soon as I can get this over with, I can get prepared for the weekend and Mecca's visit.

The interview went great. If they hire me, I wouldn't get to start until the next school year but at least I'll have something lined up. I wasn't worried about money. Just like Mr. O'Conner said the school paid me for the full school year and a hefty bonus to ensure I wouldn't sue. Today is Friday, finally. I was looking forward to seeing Mecca tonight. I tried to ask Bella if she wanted to do a double date with Aspen, but she said no way. Bella's last relationship left her funny about committing to anyone else. She has her fun and that's it. I don't think she's slept with the same man twice in years. I decide what I want to wear and make plans to get my hair blown out and pressed at one of the Dominican's shops. The first time he saw me, my hair was in a wild afro twist-out. I want something different for tonight.

I walk downstairs, looking and feeling good. I'm meeting Mecca downtown because his business meeting ran long. He didn't want us to be late for the show, meeting up was the best option. I walk outside and almost trip on an envelope. I pick it up and see it has my name on it. When I open it, it's a note from Bayden.

You like playing games like a child. Walking out on me after all the things I've done for you. I made you! Since you want to be childish, I can be childish too! The perks you enjoy come with

me. If you're not with me, you don't get to enjoy the perks. Walk where you need to go, just like you walked out on me.

I look around and notice my car is gone. He took my car. I can't believe how stupid he is and how stupid he's acting. Although, the car was a gift, you don't give someone a gift and take it back. Who the fuck does that? He's such an asshole. I pull up my Uber app and get a car. I know Bayden wants to break me. Wants me to call him and curse him out but I'm not about to get down on his level. He can have that car. And he's the one calling me childish.

When I get to The Fox Theatre, I'm all up in my feelings. I'm a mixture of hurt and anger. I see Mecca standing in the lobby waiting for me. He was dressed in a button down shirt and some slacks that fit him like a glove. He was extremely handsome even with all his clothes on. I start seeing flashbacks of our night together and I remember every tattoo, every mark, every scar. I know every inch of him because I kissed and licked every inch of him. A chill runs down my back and I can feel the wetness between my legs. He gets closer to me and wraps his arms around me. His smell, his arm, his embrace puts me at ease. I want him to hold me a little longer so when he attempts to release me, I hug him tighter. I finally let him go and he pulls me close to him and lifts my chin.

"Are you ok?"

"I am, now. Come on I want to see what you picked out for me for tonight." I fake a smile to hide the pain and hurt I'm feeling.

"I figured you looked it up on your way over here. I'm glad it's still a surprise. I know you love dance, it's a special showing of Alvin Ailey Dance Company."

My hands go right to my mouth to keep me from screaming. I go to the show every year and this year I wasn't able to attend. I knew they were coming back to town but for an exclusive, private event. There were no tickets available. "How did you get tickets? This is a private event. We can't just sneak in here. Are we supposed to be here?" I start looking around and he starts laughing.

"Don't worry, if we get caught, I'll blame everything on you."

I step back and give him a look. "What?"

"Come on beautiful, give me some credit. Let's get to our seats before the show starts."

He takes my hand and guides me upstairs to the private balcony seating. I can't believe this man listened to me enough to know how much I love this show. I also can't believe he's willing to sit with me through it. I have to admit, when you see Mecca, the first thing you see is his gorgeous chocolate skin. Skin so beautiful it looks like God himself came down and kissed it into existence. His eyes greet you next, they're gray which is oddly mesmerizing because I've never seen gray eyes like his before. Our short time together before taught me he smiles at you if he likes you. If he doesn't, you're greeted with the New York mean mug. Since he likes me, I'm blessed to receive that wonderful smile and those pearly white teeth. Mecca, looks like a drug dealer however, when he opens his mouth his education and smarts catches you off guard.

When the show is over, we head over to the Museum of Art for another private party. "I love this place during the day but seeing it right now it's a different vibe." I was walking around taking in all the art on display and I turn around, Mecca and I are face to face. I didn't even realize he was that close to me.

"It's a good vibe and the beauty is unbelievable."

Clearly, he's an art lover too. "Which piece?"

"The one right in front of me."

I couldn't help but blush. I had a long talk with myself in the mirror and promised I wouldn't just spread my legs tonight. That was a lie. The intensity in his eyes has me soak and wet. Everything about tonight was about me. I've never had a date that completely centered around my enjoyment. I expressed my love of dance and art to him and he took it all in and actually listened. What man does that? I'd been with Bayden for a long time and he never planned any dates like this one. I sigh, I need to stop comparing them. They are polar opposites. "Thank you for listening to me. I don't get that often. I'm the youngest and you've met my sisters they tend to drown me out sometimes. And as far as my last relationship I feel like I wasn't heard at all. I was told my passion was a child's dream and I was too old to still be dreaming like a child. But when I see dancing like on stage tonight and when I turn around and I'm surrounded by these wonderful pieces, I know my passion is important. Thank you because that conformation was very much needed today."

"Passion is always important. It drives everything we do. You can't do anything in this life without it. Some people's passion is money. That's what drives them. They'll do anything for it. Rob, steal and kill. Shit, I've seen some people cross their own mama to get to money. And because money is their passion they don't understand when someone wants to pursue something that maybe doesn't bring them as much money. They don't understand the satisfaction. They just don't get it."

He takes my hands and brings me closer to him. He caresses my cheek; my body temperature goes up immediately. He's staring at me with those beautiful soul piercing eyes. "I know." Those are the only words I could say because I could feel myself getting ready to tear up.

"I hear you Journi. I hear you loud and clear. I see you. I see your vision too."

He places a kiss on my forehead, then he kisses my eyes and each cheek. When he reaches my lips, I swear I just melt in his arms. Being with him takes away all the things that are wrong in my world. He makes me feel, right. "Mecca."

"Damn, the way you say my name drives me crazy. Stay with me tonight. Let me make whatever happened today before you got here better. Don't say no. I just want to be near you."

I couldn't say no. "Yes." It came out as just a sultry whisper, but I know he heard me loud and clear. His arms were around my waist and we start moving through the halls toward the exit. I don't think I'll ever be able to say no to those eyes, to this feeling or to him.

Chapter 8

I Don't Do Singles

Bella

Alexa play. . . DJ Khaled. . .Wild Thoughts

Dressed in my naughty little Red Riding Hood outfit or at least that's what I call it. It's a red mesh see through jumpsuit. I head over to one of the exclusive black swinger's clubs in Atlanta. This was something I would never tell my sisters about. They know I'm freaky but not belonging to a club freaky. I know Journi would understand but not Karm. She tends to be a little judgmental. I've belonged to this club for a while now. I like it because it's clean, anything goes and everybody in here is fine as fuck. And I mean everybody, the men and the women. I think that's why they request a picture before they grant you access. I was looking for Shay tonight. She's a regular like me. I need a release and she knows exactly how to give it to me. Since the trip a couple of weekends ago I haven't felt right. Aspen had popped in my mind more than a few times. Which is crazy because I'm a hit it and quit it type of girl. He's called and even sent me a few texts. I text him back if I'm bored but I don't accept any of the phone calls. There's a simple reason for that, I don't do relationships.

My last relationship was crazy enough to sour me on all commitments. It's the typical story guy meets girl. They fall in love. I give everything to a man I thought was perfect. I do any and everything for him. I even let him convince me to let my best friend join us in a threesome. That was a big mistake. They started seeing each other behind my back. A few months later I was walking down the aisle with my sisters at their wedding. We weren't a part of the wedding party. We were going to kick his ass and hers. I wasn't just hurt, I was traumatized. Needless to say, I not only have trust issues, commitment issues but also resentment issues. That was six years ago. I heard they had two kids together, bought a house, had the perfect family until karma kicked in the door. She caught him cheating on her, no surprise there. They got divorced. She made a few attempts to contact me to apologize. I told her to miss me with that bullshit. She was only sorry because she got served what she had dished out in life.

After that situation I wanted to regain my power. I do little things to protect myself. I try not to sleep with a guy more than once. Unless the dick is good. After my little jail incident, I learned to let good dick go and move on. Now I only sleep with guys who are dogs or who understand that I require a threesome. I don't just sleep with them alone. That leads to feelings and feelings lead to situations. I'm okay with sharing because I understand I would be sharing without my permission on the back end anyway. This way I control the situation by picking the woman and the man of my liking. I protect myself because I'm allowing it to happen. I'm in control. This way there are no feelings involved, and everyone gets to walk away satisfied. I get a nut, my lady for the night gets a nut and some lucky guy gets to live out his dream of having two bad bitches in his bed for the night.

I take a seat at the bar. Aspen pops in my head again. He was just what I like in a man, handsome, sexy and dangerous. It's been a long time since a man has made me feel something. Sex with him was well, something. It was mind blowing. He's an attentive lover. His dick is so good, it could become addictive. As much as want him again, I have no intention of sleeping with him again. I just need to get laid, to get him off my mind. Sipping my drink at the bar I turn around to see who is in the club tonight. I spy with my little eye all type of goodies. There's some sexy ass men and women in here tonight. I spot Shay walking in the door like she owns the place. She is beautiful. I watch her just for minute. She's working the room. When she sees me, she licks her lips and heads my way.

"It's always a pleasure seeing you here Bella."

"You too Shay."

"That red on you is beautiful." She takes a seat next to me. "Which one of these cuties gets the pleasure of our company tonight?"

I glance around the room again; I didn't want any of these men tonight. My body was craving him. I shake it off. And then, I get a text from Aspen. He's saved in my phone as a reminder.

Don't do it: I'm at Magic City come through.

I know I shouldn't, but I want to so bad. "Nothing is catching my eye. You want to go to Magic City. Something is there that's extremely bad, but it makes me feel so damn good."

"Dick that good, it's calling you. Totally not you."

"I know. It's just." I can't explain it. I don't know how to say I'm craving his touch. Craving his lips on mine. Craving his smell and the sound of his voice. A voice that had the power to make me cum when he moaned my name. I bite my lip and cross my legs just thinking about it. Shay gently slides her hands between my legs.

"Let's go. If he has the power to get you this wet. I want to feel it too!"

Just like that we jump in my car and head over to Magic City. The ride is quiet. I'm glad she doesn't ask me any questions. Shay and I have been meeting at the club for a year. She's become a good friend that understands my needs and doesn't judge me. When we get to the club it's packed. It's the weekend which is usual for this place. When Shay and I walk in all eyes are on us. Shay nods at a few of the dancers. I spot Aspen, just seeing him takes my breath away. "He's in VIP." He's surrounded by a few guys but none of them compare to him. They all have dancers giving them lap dances but not him. He was sitting back sipping on his drink.

"The one with all the tats, right?"

"Yes, that's him." My voice was course and weak. This is not me.

"He has your ass unable to speak and shit. This is going to be fun."

We walk toward the section and Aspen's eyes fall on me. The room is crowded, the music was bumping, none of that matters, I only see and feel him. I try to shake it off again. I have to because his cocky ass will see it.

"I was waiting on you to text me back."

"I figured I'd just show up." He hugs me and he smells good. His embrace feels good too. "This is my friend Shay."

"Welcome Shay." He was speaking to her, but his eyes were only on her for just a second. They were right back on me. "Stop undressing me with your eyes and get us a drink."

He waves for the waitress to come over and motions for his friend to move over so we can all sit down. Before I could sit, he grabs my hand and puts me on his lap. I make myself comfortable. The drinks start flowing and the night goes fast. If I even eyed a girl for a second Aspen had them to come over and give me and Shay a lap dance. I was floating on cloud nine from the drinks and weed Aspen and his friends were blowing in my direction. I feel Shay's hand on one of my thighs and Aspen's hand on the other thigh. He takes his hand and gently puts it around my neck. He brings my lips close to his and forces my mouth open. He blows the weed smoke right in my mouth. I take it all in. When his lips cover mine, Shay stands up and straddles us both. He pulls on his weed again and blows in her mouth. She turns and kisses me. I let out a soft moan. "Let's go."

"Damn right before I bend both your sexy asses over right in here."

Shay and I hop in my car and follow Aspen back to his place. I don't know if he was staying with a friend or renting an air BNB. I don't care what it is or whose place it is. I just want to feel him inside of me. We get in the room. Shay and I start kissing and undressing each other. Aspen strips down and sits on the bed watching us and stroking his dick. Damn his dick is beautiful. I walk over to him and kiss him. I turn around and sit on him in a reverse cowboy position. I slide down on his dick slowly. He's just the right size and just the right width. A width that makes my walls scream and almost makes me squirt on impact. His lays back a little and puts his hand on breast. Squeezing and massaging them. Shay comes over and bites my nipples. Her hands are on my waist guiding me up and down his dick. Her tongue travels down my body and greets my clit. She kisses it, blows on it, flicks her tongue back and forth. When she starts sucking it, I start getting wetter and wetter. Aspen puts his hand around my neck.

"Don't cum yet. Hold that shit in. Don't you cum for her. Just me."

I could feel the sweat coming from the heat rising in my body. He can't make that type of request. This feeling is euphoric. I feel my body tense up, I know the wave is coming. "I can't hold it."

"You only cum for me." He taps Shay to move. In a quick move he flips me over and starts pounding me from the back. Shay gets on the bed in front of me to allow me to feast on her. Aspen is hitting all my spots. He presses down on my back; I arch it more. He pulls out of me and runs his tongue from my ass crack to my pussy. I swear every part of me goes insane. He slams back into me, this time he takes his thumb and puts it in my ass, he then reaches his hand around my body to do the job Shay was doing. Instead of his fingers I feel a vibration that goes from slow to fast in seconds. A wave of pleasure hits me and I feel like I'm about to pass out from it.

"That's right cum on this dick."

I do just that. I cum so hard I feel like I'm gasping for air. I feel like I'm floating through space. "Aspen!"

"That pussy some good." He pulls off the condom. "Come lick this nut off me Shay."

I've never seen Shay move as quick as she was moving. Her lips were surrounding his dick in seconds. For some reason I was jealous. I want to taste him, but my legs were like noodles I couldn't move. I sit back and watch them. Aspen's eyes are on me. They are intense as fuck. Shay was giving him a good sloppy head job and he was watching me. I was attempting to control my reaction because I could see him reading me.

"She sucking your dick good. You just sitting there watching. Don't worry I won't nut for her. Just for you. Where you want this nut?"

Everything Aspen did was sexy. He's demanding and controlling. All the things I hate in a man, I was enjoying in him. I was wet all over again. My throat was dry. I couldn't force the words to come out. It's the first time my ass was speechless. I sit there looking confused because this was new for me. I'm the one that's always in control.

"Oh, you shy now. Don't pull that shit. Get over here and get your nut."

I crawl over and Shay pops him out her mouth, I put him right in mine. A few sucks in and I feel his cum in mouth, sliding down my throat. Tasting just like sweet milk to me. I look up into his eyes and he smiles. After I suck every last drop, I watch him walk into the bathroom.

Shay starts giggling like a school-girl. "Bitch you in trouble. That dick is deadly. You want me to leave?"

"No please." I didn't know what was happening to me because just for a minute I thought about saying yes but I couldn't. I don't do singles. Aspen walks out the bathroom dick hard as hell again. It was about to be a long night. I can hear Shay whisper damn and she licks her lips. She looks at me and walks over to the bed.

"She only gets this dick if you want her to get it. It's up to you because it's your dick."

I turn around and look at Shay. I hastate for a minute. *Get yourself together Bella and take some control here.* "She can have it, but don't you dare cum in her. It's for her pleasure not yours. And make that shit good. Make her cream and squirt. I want to taste it all."

"Anything you want. But don't think you're going to just sit here and watch." He lights another blunt. Takes a few pulls all while standing there looking like an African king, dick just out swinging. He's taking his time, thinking. He starts stroking his dick and smiling. I can't help but get wet all over again just off the beautiful sight standing before me. When the anticipation of what we were going to do next starts killing me, he speaks. "Shay bend over and get on them knees for me. Bella get that fine ass under Shay. You know 69 style." We both hop into position ready to go. "Bella you know this dick likes wet pussy. Wet that pussy up for me. Make that shit super wet so I can slide the fuck in there." I do exactly as he says and start licking and suck on Shay. And she starts sucking on me. When he slides into Shay, he starts hitting her with the good stroke. I can tell because she's getting wetter and creaming like crazy. Shay's a squitter but only a few men can get her to that point. Aspen was getting her there fast. When I her say she was cummin', Aspen pulls out and she gushes everywhere.

Five minutes later, Shay was passed out on her stomach sleeping. Aspen has me pinned against the wall, fucking me like we just started. He slows up for just a minute and I fell a vibration against my clit.

"I stopped at a sex store before I got in town. I couldn't stop thinking about you. Playing with toys is not my thing but I see you like what this does. Just seeing the fuck faces you make about to make me become a toy connoisseur. I see you're afraid to be with me alone, but I got everything you will need."

He was stroking me, and the vibrations was sending me into a space I didn't want to be in. I don't know when I lost control. I don't know if it was in this room or back in New Orleans. But I lost control. I know I have because I'm agreeing to just be with him. I'm enjoying us. And again, I don't do singles.

Chapter 9

No Woman Rejects Me

Bayden

Alexa play. . . Jay-Z. . . 99 Problems

Every eye in the room is on me. This feeling right here doesn't get old. I just landed a new contract with Nike worth over ten million dollars over the next five years. It's an exclusive ad deal with The Hawks and Nike. I can now work directly with the players and their agents which leads to bigger and better deals. The percentage I'm going to get for any of the deals I complete will be over the top. I'm in the position to have money on top of money. I look around the room at the smiles but behind them I could see the jealousy in their eyes. I wasn't supposed to land this deal. There were two other senior VPs ahead of me. They just didn't move as fast or as good as me. When I got wind of this deal and which partner was in charge of it, I knew exactly what I needed to do. Mr. Conrad, the partner in charge of the deal, has a very particular taste for whores. I heard he likes his sex nasty and super freaky. I heard he loves to role play as well. Who am I to judge? At a cocktail party over the weekend I made sure to bring Lena and one of her friends. Him, and most of the men at the party were drooling over Lena. I made sure she dressed the part I needed her to play. When she brushed passed him in the hallway, he almost grabbed her ass. I guess he's a supporter of 45. Just grabbing women by the pussy or the ass. I casually walked over and started making small talk with him. When he asked about Lena, I told him something could be arranged. Just like that a backroom deal was made, simple and easy. If only Lena and her friend knew their pussies were worth over ten million.

Lena was upset and angry she had to sleep with that old, white, nasty bastard. I presented the bigger picture to her. I explained how this would lead to her being in more ads and getting bigger and better deals. After all Nike is a worldwide company. When I sent her a new Birkin bag, she got over that shit right away. A bag I basically regifted. Journi had left it in one of the downstairs closets. I gave it to her last Christmas. She said she liked it, but she didn't even bother taking it out the box. She was always fussing about me spending too much money on her. About how she couldn't carry that type of purse to her job at the school because she didn't want to be judged. That's something that will never come out of Lena's mouth. The more money I spend the wider her legs and mouth opens.

Just thinking about Journi had me missing her. I walk back to my office and call my secretary to ask her did she have Journi's car picked up over the weekend. She assures me it's done. I tell her to contact the car company to make sure it was done. She comes back into my office and tells me the car was picked up on Friday. If the car was picked up on Friday, why haven't I heard from Journi yet? She should be mad and upset with me. Upset enough to call or come see me. That hasn't happened yet. The thing about Journi I used to admire was her double sided personality. She had her passive side. That side of her hates conflict unless her ghetto ass sisters pulled her into their mess. They were good at dragging her into their problems. Then there was that fire side. That side came out doing and after arguments. When she was worked up and angry, she would pour all that passion into me. When she's passionate about things she puts her heart and soul into everything. When she was like that she would let go in the bedroom. Just thinking about that passion had my dick hard. Usually when we have a bad argument, I could send her some her flowers. Promise to spend more time with her. Make her a priority over work. This time was different. I knew she would be upset but I didn't think she would be upset enough to move out. No one walks away from me. I figured I'd teach her ass a lesson. She's been out of my life for almost a month and I want her back. She belongs to me. I made her into the woman she is today. Everything about her belongs to me.

I take the chance and go over to her sister's place. I'm hoping those two bitches are not there. When the door opens Journi is standing there in a tank top and some booty shorts absolutely glowing. This wasn't how she was supposed to look. She should still be crying her eyes out over me. Over the car. "You're looking beautiful today."

"What do you want Bayden?"

"I want to know what happened."

"What do you mean what happened? You know what happened. Why are you here? Do you want the other things you gave me back?"

There's that fire I enjoy. Making up will be good. "I'm sorry. I shouldn't have taken the car back, but you forced my hand."

"I forced your hand. You're such a fucking narcissist blaming me for something you did."

"What did I do Journi that was so bad? I loved you and treated you good. I made sure you had the best of everything. The only thing I'm guilty of is working too much and not giving you the attention you want all the time."

"Attention? Is that what you think I want? Attention! I wanted your time. I wanted you to stop trying to change me. I wanted you to stop fucking with them hoes. But you couldn't do any of that. Why are you here? I'm not what you want."

"You're everything I want." I step closer to her to grab her hand, but she moves back. "Journi, don't let what we had end over one disagreement."

"It's not just one disagreement. It's you choosing to spend time with that internet slut over me. It's you choosing your job over me. It's you trying to change me all the damn time. Judging my family. Judging me."

I step closer to her and grab the sides of her arms. I don't do good with taking no for an answer. "Journi, just listen." A voice comes from behind me and a hand is on my shoulder almost making me fall backwards.

"Son, take your hands off of her."

I turn around and it's a big black thug looking dude. He was looking at me like he was about to kill me. It figures he would live in this neighborhood. This is a hood ass area of town. He's probably one of her sister's boyfriends. He looks like something Bella would bring home. "This has nothing to do with you. Mind your business."

"Fuck you mean mind my business. She is my business."

What does he mean she's his business? He has the nerve to get all up in my face. Just like a street nigga. All they know how to do is fight. "Like I said this has nothing to do with you."

"Maybe you don't hear too good. Let me make it clear right now."

Journi steps between us. "Mecca, it's fine. I got it. Can you wait inside?"

"Nah, I'll wait right here. I'll keep my cool for you, right now."

Journi turns and looks at me. "It's best you go Bayden. You and I have nothing else to discuss."

This doesn't make sense. I know she didn't move on this damn fast. Not with this thug. "Are you kidding me? You're with this street nigga now? It figures. I tried to give your hood rat ass a better life. But I see the finer things in life aren't for you. You bitches are all the same. You can't appreciate an educated, employed black man. The ones that work hard to earn a living. You would rather a dirty, grimy hustler."

"My dude you talking a lot shit. But you don't know me to even speak on me. I'm keeping my cool for her. Keep talking and I'll show you just how dirty and grimy I am."

I look at Journi and shake my head. All the things I've done for her over the years. All the doors I opened for her. I walk back to my car pissed off. I can't believe her. Ghetto bitch! I tried to introduce her to the finer things in life, but she just crawled right back into the hood. No woman rejects me and disrespects me. I'll teach her ass a lesson she'll never forget. She'll have no other choice but to come crawling her ass back to me.

Chapter 10

Half in and Half Out

Karman

Alexa play. . . Young Jeezy . . . Leave You Alone

I adjust myself in my chair. I've been sitting in my office looking over three properties I need to sell for over an hour. I had a few deals on the table but they didn't come through. The last two investors suddenly became cash strapped. I need to get these properties sold right away. I haven't made a sale in the past two months. The head bosses in my firm were starting to doubt my ability to do well in commercial real estate. I'm not crazy, I know what's been going on around here. One of the boss' son started working here a few months ago. He was the new golden boy around the office. I've been watching them give him first choice at all the great properties and everyone else gets what's left. It's easy to sell a building in Buckhead. I should be listing those properties after all the hard work I've done around here. I made this company over twenty million dollars this past year. I fought to get this top spot in the office and now they're just handing it to junior on a silver platter.

I'm better than him I know it. I just need to find the right investors for these listings. Looking over the pictures the buildings aren't very appealing. Maybe I should go out there and take better pictures. The ones my assistant took are showing everything at a bad angle. I pack up and head over to the buildings. The sun is starting to set making it a great back drop for the buildings. Reviewing the pictures, I realize how much better these are compared to the others. I need to get them uploaded and sent to some other investors I know that are looking to expand. When I turn around Legend is leaning against my car smiling. I bite my lip to hold in my smile. "What are you doing here?"

"Checking out the view. And daddy likes what he sees."

He's such an ass. If he could only keep his mouth closed it would be so much better. "How did you find me?"

"Since you weren't answering my calls or texts, I called your office. I took one of your business cards. Your assistant told me where you would be."

I smirk walking pass him. I was impressed that he thought enough of me to even look me up. "What do you want?" He grabs my waist and pulls me close to him. He sneaks a kiss on my neck.

"I wanted to see you. Come on let's get something to eat."

Legend is far from my type. He's uncultured and untamed. He's loud and obnoxious. He doesn't play by rules because he's arrogant and creates his own rules. And worst of all I know he's in the street. But there's something about him that intrigues me. Not to mention how handsome his ass is. He has this dark chocolate skin that I swear doesn't have a single blemish or mark on it. It's just smooth. His hair is in locs, which he's wearing neatly braided to the back. He really isn't my type but here I find myself sitting across the table from him laughing at all his corny jokes.

"You seem like you got something on your mind today. What's going on?"

"It's just a work thing. You know I worked hard to get to where I am only for some catered to, privilege bastard to come and get ahead of me."

"I'll be honest. I don't know that many black women in commercial real estate. It's usually white men."

"I know. It's an all-white boys club. But I broke into it. And I'm good at it. I'm really good. Wait, what do you know about commercial real estate?"

"Oh, I forgot, I'm supposed to be a dumb thug."

"I didn't say that."

"You didn't need to say it. It's how you treat me. You know how you picked this spot over here on the south side when I suggested we go to Lenox to eat. How you keep looking around to make sure no one sees you with me."

I was ashamed, why the hell was I acting this way? "I'm sorry. It's just my image is everything especially right now."

"What's the end result?"

"Result of what?"

"Of you getting into their world. Pretending to assimilate as one of them. What satisfaction will you get?"

"Assimilate? Ok with the big words."

"Just answer the question."

"The satisfaction of knowing I did it. Most people don't understand it. My mom, was this brilliant woman, she was a genius with numbers. She could have been an engineer designing aerospace ships for NASA. She wasn't. She allowed the people around her to keep her in this box and convince her she couldn't rise above what they imagined for her. She became a teacher and worked nights at a hotel doing accounting work for them. I saw it in her eyes whenever my sisters or I reached a new level that she was enjoying it just as much as us because she didn't let herself get to those levels.

I promised myself that wouldn't be me. I won't let anyone put me in a box and say what I can't do. The more they tell me I can't do it, the more I want to prove them wrong. The more they say a woman can't, I do. When they say a black woman can't do it, I do. When they say that hood bitch is not good enough, I prove I am."

"We're more alike than you understand. I don't want anyone boxing me in either. I get it. Just don't lose yourself. Learn what you need to learn from them and build your own shit. That way you're free to be you without the stress."

What he said was true. Some days I do feel like I'm losing myself in that office. Being the only black woman in there is hard and lonely. "I'll keep that in mind. But right now, I refuse to let that prep school reject win."

"You want me to kill him?"

I almost spit out my drink. I start waving my hands. "No. I got it for now."

"Send the property listing and pictures to me when you get the pictures up. I know a few investors."

I start laughing, "I need investors not dealers."

"Cause I'm street that's all I know. There you go, putting me in a box. I'm a hustler but I'm about my business too. In fact, most days business is the only thing that matters. I know some people. Don't always judge a book by the cover baby girl."

He winks at me tosses some money on the table for the tab and we head out. "Let me take you somewhere."

"Take me where? Let me find out you know Atlanta better than me."

Legend takes my hand and proceeds to take us to downtown Atlanta. We walk through Centennial Olympic Park. Just like the night I meet him in New Orleans, our conversation just flows. Although he seems one dimensional. He has this understanding of life and things that's multifaceted. We end up riding Skyview Atlanta. The city looks beautiful from up here. While I'm looking at the view Legend comes behind me and wraps his arms around me. He smells good and I can't help but melt into his body. He turns me around and our eyes meet. His eyes are warm and caring not at all what you would expect on a person like him. He leans down, lowers his head and smiles that cocky smile of his. All night I've found my admiring his grill that covers just his fangs. It's thuggish and childish but on him it's sexy. I can't help how turned on I feel by him. He puts his hands on the window, on each side of me, trapping me underneath him. I take a moment and take in everything about him. He has this perfect frame, it's muscular but not thick. His jawline is strong, and that beard and those locs, just work on him. Why is he looking at me like that? He licks my lips. My legs start shaking. He smiles that cocky smile again.

"I want to lick every damn part of you."

His words came out soft but strong. They were strong enough to create a poodle between my legs. My breathing starts to increase. "Umm." I was speechless. When his lips cover mine and his starts sucking on my bottom lip, I don't know what to do. The care he's taken to make this feel good is crazy. I haven't felt this feeling in a long time. He pulls back and I catch my breath. "Legend." This time he leans over me and nibbles on my ear.

"Call my name like that again and I won't be able to control myself."

Fuck the good girl, reserved shit. I haven't had dick in a long time. "Legend." In a second, he was pulling up my skirt and ripping off my panties and unbuckling his belt. I didn't wait, I unbuttoned his jeans and pull them down. I wrap my legs around his waist. When he enters me, I almost scream. He wasn't even all the way in, yet. His dick is thick and long. My nails are digging deeper and deeper into his arms with each inch he gives to me. "Oh shit."

"This pussy tight baby girl. You a virgin?"

"It's been a minute."

"I like that. You was saving it for a nigga like me. Don't worry I got you."

When he said that he pins me against the glass and starts stroking me slow and steady. I wrap my arms around his neck. His fingers are tracing the tattoos that are each one of my thighs.

"I been wanting to touch these mother fuckers since the night of the party. They sexy as hell sitting on these thick, pretty ass thighs."

I don't know if it was the altitude we were at or the motion in his stroke or the shit he was saying. But my head is spinning. He's whispering my name and biting my neck and kissing my lips. I could feel the heat between us. My orgasm was coming, as much as I want to stop it, I welcome it. When it hits, it's like a wave of water crashing into rocks on the beach. I can't move. He keeps going hitting a spot that sends another wave of emotions over me and I cum again. I was calling his name, begging him to stop before he hit my spot again. I had never been this wet before in my life. He didn't stop, in fact he laid on my spot like it was home to him.

"It's too wet. I'm about to nut."

I feel him jerk. I start removing my legs from around his waist, they feel like jelly. I stumble but he catches me. I'm at a loss for words about my behavior. I look around and remember where we are and wonder if someone saw us. "I can't believe we just did that. I hope no one saw us."

"Don't worry I paid for the box car in front and behind us. I also paid the ride operator to hold us up here a little longer than normal."

"Damn, I hate being predictable." I reach for my panties, but he snatches them out my hand, sniffs them and puts them in his pocket.

"Far from it. I believe in putting what I want in the atmosphere. I'm feeling you Karman. I mean really feeling you. I'm a Legend baby, I don't chase. But for you I will. Feel me."

I just nod my head. On the ride back to my car I'm in head thinking about what I've done and how I've opened myself up when I shouldn't have. He takes my hand and kisses it.

"You over there thinking about this dick. Or just over thinking what happened?"

"Let me tell you a story. When I was in my teens, I started dating this guy. We were all in love. You know that teenage love you feel will last forever. He was like you, half in the streets and half out. Senior year we're filling out college apps and I'm excited because finally I could be at ease knowing he was safe and away from that life. We both applied to FAMU. He called me and told me he received his letter and I had also received mine. We both were accepted. He was coming over to take me out to celebrate. He never made it. He made a stop to drop off some weight and they shot him because a key was missing. They thought he was trying to get over on them. But the key had fallen in his trunk. I had to walk across the stage the next week with his picture because we promised to do it together." I wipe the tears from my eyes. "It's not that I don't like you. It's that I can't like you. Thanks for tonight. Lose my number." Before he could grab my arm, I was out of his car and walking swiftly to mine. I wasn't about to allow myself to catch any feelings for him. I can't risk it. In life you can't straddle the fence. Either you're in or you're out. He got his dick wet and I got several nuts. That's exactly where we leave it.

Chapter 11

It's Pleasure, Not Business

Mecca

Alexa play. . .Roddy Rich. . .High Fashion

Standing outside a building, I turn to check out the neighborhood. I can tell it's what people would call an up and coming area because of all the abandon properties around it. It's actually Gentrification. The building looks better in pictures than it does in person. I like that. I don't want anything pretty. I look over at Aspen. He isn't saying much which is a first. "What do you think?"

"It's old and dirty."

"I don't want something shiny and new."

"But we can afford shiny and new."

"We can afford this whole city. Doesn't mean I want to buy it." A car pulls up and I see Karman getting out.

"What are you guys doing here? I have a meeting with some very important clients?"

Aspen looks her up and down. "What are we chop liver?"

I can see she's about to go off. "Karman, we are your clients. Can you take us inside? Let me see what the floor plan looks like."

"Listen if you are wasting my time."

Aspen starts to get impatient. "Does it look like we stand around wasting time?"

She looks from him to me. "You don't have to get snappy about it. Come on, let me take you on a tour?"

"Aspen, I doubt she understands that we can buy this. She doesn't know us like that."

"Bella told me she was bougie. I didn't believe her. Watch this." He catches up with Karman. "Mrs. Fields, since we're clients put on your professional voice for us. We expect a grand professional tour as well."

Karman turns around and shoots him a look. "Yep, you and Bella are perfect for each other."

Walking inside of the building it was very different from the outside. It was ten floors of beautiful office space. It was modern and up to date. "What do you think Aspen?"

"I like this shit. It's ugly as fuck on the outside but it's modern in here. The space is big enough to bring our full-time workers in house. But gives us enough room to hire more. You know when you first said we should start thinking about a home base, I figured you were going crazy. I see it. I see the full potential in here. I also see me sitting in one of these big ass offices barking out orders."

I do a double take at him. "Who said you get the big office? That's reserved for me."

"No, that office is reserved for a boss like me."

Karman walks over to us. "There are four offices up here that are the same size. What you guys can do is knock down the walls and make the space bigger. That way each of you will get an office that's the same size."

"I like that idea Karman. Aspen you can take the two offices on that end and I can take the two on this end. While we are redecorating, I want this space minimal. Reserved for us and clients only. We'll need to frost up the glass surrounding the conference room for privacy purposes."

"Good idea Mecca. I want to put a state of the art audio, video system in there. I get sick of showing our video footage on those cheap film projectors. I want those criminals on a big screen like we're at the movies."

"Criminals! Wait what is it you guys do?"

"We own a private security firm." Karman looks a little surprise.

"I want a floor for just my lab, Mecca. I swear I wasn't feeling this shit at first, but I could get into it. No more hauling equipment state to state and working at whatever tech lab we could rent out or a trailer. It can be my own design. I can buy that new shit I been eyeing for over a year now. I didn't get it because I didn't have a place to put it."

Aspen was spinning around all excited. We had been fighting laying down roots for a while, but now seems like the perfect time to do it. We were coming to Atlanta to do three jobs but ended up with ten other jobs. That's enough to keep us busy for the rest of the year. We can still take on jobs out of state, but this will be our home base. "Karman did you bring all the paperwork? I want to get this signed tonight. I know a great architect out in New York. I can have him bring his crew out next week to get to work designing everything."

"Don't you want to know the price?"

"Mrs. Fields if we need to ask the price than we couldn't afford it."

"Aspen you have one more time to play with me."

"Now that's not at all professional, *Ms. Fields*."

I was cracking up at how Aspen and Karman were going back and forth. "Don't mind him, get the paperwork so we can get this started."

"I'll have to thank Journi for letting you guys know about this property. I appreciate the business."

I step to reply but Aspen pushes me out the way. "No let me do the honors Mecca. It wasn't Journi. It was your boo, Legend. Why don't you call him and thank him."

Now Aspen knew full well that she told Legend they couldn't be together. We had a sit down with him last weekend and he was pretty upset about it. That's another reason why Aspen is going hard on her. Although Legend is still in the street, he's a good person. He took care of me and Aspen like we were family from day one. He does that with everyone he knows. If he likes you. He makes sure you're good. I brought up an idea about opening up a home base location and Legend immediately told us about this space. He told us the hard time Karman's firm was giving her. He said if we didn't get it, he would get it just to help her out. I can tell he's feeling her more than he's willing to admit. Nobody drops almost half a million for a property they won't use.

Karman gets all the paperwork together and I make a call to my accountant Paige and her husband Pharaoh. They are one dynamic duo. She protects and makes me money and he's about to create the office of my dreams. We sign all the paperwork and Karman hands over the keys to us. "It's been a pleasure doing business with you Karman."

"It's been a pleasure with you Mecca, I wish I could say the same for Aspen's ass."

Aspen signed his name and left about five minutes ago. "Legend is like Aspen's big brother. He admires him and looks up to him a lot. He knows like I know that Legend was a little hurt by you rejecting him."

"Did he say that?"

A look of concern crosses her face. "He didn't need to say it. We know it. I'll be honest. Legend is loud and obnoxious. He is the life of the party. If there's no party, he'll make it a party. His path in life hasn't been clean cut but he has a good heart. Not only that he's smart and he knows enough to walk away before it's too late."

"It's complicated. I just can't take that chance."

"Matters of the heart usually are complicated."

"What about you and Journi?"

At the mention of her name I can't help but smile. "I like your sister. She's a beautiful person."

"I like her with you. She seems like herself again. Don't hurt her. She's been hurt enough. Her ex is a piece of shit that used and abused her in more ways than one. Even now that they've broke up, he's still trying to break her."

Now she had my full attention. The short time I've been with Journi she's been nothing but sweet and loving. I've fallen head over heels for her. Lately I've notice her pulling away, I've been wondering why. "Trying to break her? What is he doing?"

"She hasn't told you anything?"

"No."

"Maybe, I shouldn't say anything, but fuck him. He took her car. He's maxed out some of her credit cards. And he keeps calling her day and night from different numbers. He's just trying to break her but she's doing her best to stay strong. I know that's because of the joy you've been bringing to her life. Just don't hurt her or me and Bella will beat your ass too! We're just waiting to do a pop up on his ass."

"Calm down. A pop up won't be needed. Besides if you or Bella get one scratch on you, Legend and Aspen will go to war over you two."

"Don't worry we are good at fighting our own battles."

I walk her out the building and back to her car. I want to tell her they didn't have any battles anymore, but I think me saying we have their back will be too much for her to understand. We'll just have to show them. I text a few of my staff and Aspen. I want to know everything about Journi's ex. I hate a weak man that can't just walk away when a relationship is over. Since he enjoys breaking people, I'll introduce him to the master at breaking people.

Chapter 12

I Am Who I Am

Legendary "Legend" Johnson

Alexa play. . .Jacquees'. . . Who's

Each puff of smoke was easing my mind. Things have been heavy lately. The moves I'm making will either set me free or cost me everything. It's a risk I'm willing to take. The pressure to get everything done was on my back but this process can't be rushed. Rome wasn't built in a day. Uncertainty is something I'm not good at dealing with. I'm a man who doesn't sit around and wait on anyone to make things happen; I do that shit myself. This waiting on people and things is new to me. I take my phone and scroll until I find Karman's page. Looking at her page, I admire the way she conducts herself. All of her pictures are classy and tasteful. She's always well dressed and barely showing any skin. Even all covered up I can see her beauty. She is stunning and captivating. Those deep almond shape eyes and those voluptuous lips give her this unique look. At first glance she wasn't my type. Had I run up on her in Atlanta, I would have looked at that ass and kept it moving. She's in straight business mode out here all the time. The Karman I met in New Orleans was open and free. There was this spark in her eyes that attracted me to her. That or maybe it was the thigh tattoos that was on full display at her cousin's party. With her wearing less than nothing I got to see the piece of her she was trying not to show the world. That was the piece of her that I found the most attractive. Carefully drawn on each one of her thighs was different works of art. And I'm not talking about little butterflies or paws. These were full thigh covering pieces of places and words in beautiful, bright colors. I know because I couldn't keep my eyes off of them the whole night. Instead of sitting across from me, I wanted them wrapped around me. That didn't happen that night, instead we ended up sitting on the roof of my car out by the lake, eating crawfish and crab legs. We did a lot of talking and laughing. We talked about everything, life, tv, politics, just anything that came to mind. It was refreshing to be with a woman that could hold my attention mentally. People see the outside of me and judge me on just my looks and loudness. They don't know I hold a master's degree in business, and I have a minor in psychology. She didn't know either. I want her to like me for me not for anything else.

I exhale and close my eyes. The image of her appears. I can feel my hands holding her fine ass up against the glass the last night I saw her. I've been craving to trace all those tattoos and I had finally gotten my chance. The way she was fighting me and flirting with me at the same time had me beyond turned on. I felt like a lion chasing prey. Except the prey was toying with me. When I finally trapped her the way her body responded to my touch was incredible. She was so fucking tight and wet. My thoughts were interrupted by an alarm going off in front me. I was in the security room of my house out in Stockbridge. A few minutes away from Atlanta. I purchased this property years ago and Aspen and Mecca hooked me up with a top of the line special design security system. No one but me and them knew about this room. I focus on the monitor that's in front of me and watch Swiss move from room to room checking for me. I click a button on the remote that starts the shower in my master bathroom. I watch as he puts his ear to the door for a minute and then walks in the room. Instead of calling my name he walks in and starts going through my things. I sit up in my chair and watch what comes next. He goes to my closet continuing his search. I don't know what he's trying to find. When he leaves out the room, he pulls his phone out and makes a call.

I've known Swiss since we were kids growing up in the projects of New York. When we jumped off the porch, we did it together. I made sure whenever I got, he got too! We used to move so tight together people thought we were brothers. A few years ago, Swiss started moving funny. He started making decisions without discussing anything with me. I started hearing rumors he was ready to take over what we built together. I paid it no mind, niggas always talking shit. But if nothing my study of the human brain taught me, it taught me to trust my instincts when it comes people. Also, to watch before acting. That's what I've been doing, watching him. People are like lab rats. Put them in a controlled environment and they will show you exactly what you need to know.

I walk downstairs and find Swiss playing the game with another member of my crew. "Who down here winning?"

Swiss turns around and smiles. "You know I am. He don't know nothing about this damn Madden."

"Your ass always talking shit." The game ends and Swiss jumps up.

"I'm talking shit because I can always back that shit up. Now that I'm finish playing these games and schooling these niggas let me holla at you for minute."

"What's good?"

"What's good is we been here for a week and haven't met with the connect yet. We need to get at him and get this deal taken care of like now. I'm ready to go back to New York and take over the rest of the territories like I been saying."

"I told you I'm not trying to start a war. You need to slow down."

"Slow down. Nigga in this business there is no slowing down. You either on go or you get gone. Don't you remember, you taught me that."

"I also taught you to not do unnecessary shit."

"That bougie bitch got you going soft. She got you chasing her ass when you should be chasing this paper."

Before he could say another word, my hands were around his neck. I slam him against the wall and increase my gripe. "Say I'm soft again. Say it cause, I don't think I heard you right." Two of my team and Mecca starts pulling me off of him. He stands there looking at me, holding his throat, looking like he's about to reach for his gun. "Pull that gun and you better shoot to kill."

"You doing to much as usual Legend. You willing to ruin years of friendship over a bitch that don't even want your dumb ass."

I was trying to run up on him again but Mecca's ole strong ass had me wrapped up.

"Let's take a ride Legend."

"Go ahead and take that ride with Mecca. You need to roll out the game and retire like his punk ass. He ain't about no money either. He's only about cock blocking. If I had got to that fine ass bitch Journi she would be in here right now sucking this dick."

I feel Mecca release me and run up on Swiss and give him a quick two piece. Now it was me trying to hold Mecca back. The difference is he's strong as ox. And as quiet as he is, Mecca is crazy as fuck. He was giving Swiss the business in here. When we finally pull him off Swiss; Swiss looks like he went twelve rounds in the ring. Mecca doesn't even have a scratch on him. "Come on Mecca, let's take that ride." I turn around and give Swiss a smirk. I told his ass a long time ago to stop fucking with Mecca. Lesson learned the hard way. "Be gone when I get back. Since you ready to be back in New York go ahead and make that happen. I got down here covered." I pull Mecca out the door.

"Tell me why you still deal with him?"

"We been friends for as long as I can remember. We started in this game together. I guess it's loyalty to a fault."

"That loyalty is going to cost you. He's a jealous as nigga and always has been. Even back in the day. That shit didn't just start."

"I know you never liked him." After meeting Mecca and Aspen in juvie and we got released. I brought them on our team. They worked hard. Aspen had the ability to set up a perimeter that was basically tight. He had the northern trap set up like southern trap houses. The difference is he had it on open streets in the middle of New York. Mecca was quick with figuring out how to get the product handed off without him or Aspen even touching the shit. They made money on top of money. Not only that if anyone got out of hand Mecca took care of it with a quickness. He looks quiet. But we called him a quiet storm. He would body a nigga with the quickness. Just like tonight. If he really wanted to kill Swiss. Swiss would be dead. Aspen would be bringing in a clean up to dispose of the body.

"It wasn't about liking him. I wasn't trying to date his ass. It was about trust and when he stole from you that first time and tried to blame us, he showed his hand. After that you blew it off, but I kept an eye on him."

"I should have listened to you back then." Mecca gets really quiet and his jaw gets tight. He's humble. A characteristic I always liked about him. Had I said this shit to Aspen, he would have gloated all in my face. "I heard some rumors a few years back. I paid it no mind. But I started watching my back. I've had heat on me lately. Some spots been raided, and I got money and product coming up missing left and right. I feel like I've had eyes on me a lot lately. I caught him in my room tonight searching my shit." Mecca looks at me out the side of his eye.

"You need my services?"

"I don't want him dead yet. I need to know what he's been up to. I need to know who he's been talking to. Lately he's been trying to talk with my connect alone. But you know Fire and Jaivon don't talk to anybody but me. Besides on a trip to New York, he met Fire and rubbed him the wrong way."

"What his ass do?"

"He said some slick shit to Fire. He was completely unaware that he was our connect. Fire was about to light his ass up."

"Yeah, he crazier than me."

"That's up for debate. Both of y'all got some damn screws loose."

"Fuck you. I ain't that damn crazy. That nigga be burning people alive and shit. I just kill them."

"You act like it's different."

"It will be my pleasure to look into that nigga for you." Mecca gets quiet. "The property was nice. I got it. Aspen was fighting that shit at first. But the more he walked around and looked, the more he felt it. He picked out a whole floor for his lab.

He went out today and got one of them white coats and got his name on it. He's excited."

"Karman sent me a thank you text. I told her ass; she owes me dinner."

"She fighting you and Bella is fighting Aspen. Looks like I lucked up and got the one sister that is open and ready for something real."

"Karman is ready too she just don't know a nigga like me don't give up that damn easy. And I always get what I want. It's a big move. Buying this space. It means you putting roots down. You like her that much?"

"I do but it's not about her. I'm sick of all the traveling. I just want to sit my ass down sometimes. I thought about coming back to New York, but I can't."

"You know you will have to face the music at one point in time." Mecca has spent years on the road running from a situation that should have been handled a long time ago. He still wasn't ready to face it. But the day will come when we will have to face the music. We all do. When those shadows from our past come walking through, we all have to face them."

Chapter 13

I'll Protect You

Mecca

Alexa play. . . Stokley. . .She

Walking into the office I was amazed at how fast the renovations were completed. Them fools working for Pharaoh must be scared as hell of him. In four weeks, he took this building and transformed it into a newly, state of the art, hi-tech office. We kept the outside the same only cleaning it. We weren't worried about anybody breaking in because we have cameras and sensors. We just prefer to hide in plain sight.

"I can't believe this is all ours. Tell me again why it took this long for us to lay roots?"

Aspen comes in the door of my office, stands in front and turns around showing off his lab coat that I've already seen over a million times before he takes a seat. He was correct, the office was nice. Too nice for words. It was amazing and he's right it was all ours. We spared no expense to do everything our way. "We didn't need it before. But now is the perfect time to put down roots."

"Are we still talking about business or is this about your relationship?"

"A little of both. I feel like Atlanta is a hot spot of mess and disfunction. We can make a killing here."

"You got that right. I ran some stats on company theft in the past five years within a 100 mile radius and it's through the roof.

We could eat off this area alone for the rest of our lives. Besides roots can be a good thing. I think it's a smart move."

"Now are you talking business or relationship?"

Aspen shakes his head. "There's no relationship."

"Is it just a thing? Because I haven't seen you with anyone else."

"Believe me it's been a few others. Bella has made sure of it."

He smirks and I give him a look. "I'm not sure I understand."

"It's complicated. Bella is complicated. She has a wall built up. I've never seen a woman as guarded as her. It's a battle. I don't even know if it's worth it."

I've known Aspen for years. If he's interested in a woman, it's a big deal. He's just accustomed to women chasing him and not the other way around. "I don't think I've ever seen you run from a fight."

"Who said I was running?"

I lean back in my chair and raise my eyebrows. "It just sounded like you were giving up."

"I'm not giving up. I'm just saying. Fuck, I don't know what I'm saying. She has me all twisted and confused. She pushes all my buttons and gets under my skin with her need to control everything."

"Someone who likes to be in complete control. I can't imagine such a person." The more I learn about Bella, the more I understand, she's just like Aspen. They both seem like control freaks. They are both fighting each other. In order for them to work one person will need to relinquish control. A call from the security desk lets me know I have a visitor. We both glance at the security camera. It's Journi. I tell him to let her up.

I can't help but watch her as she glides down the hallway. She's wearing a maxi dress that's hugging all her curves. Her hair is up. She looks like a kid exploring a playground. She looks at everything, running her fingers across the desks and spinning around like she doesn't have a care in the world. I could watch her all day and never get bored. Each step has her hips swaying to a beat only she can hear. Whatever melody it is has me hypnotized. It should be a crime for a woman to be that damn fine. She's smiling and that makes me smile.

"I don't think I've ever seen the great Mecca smile as much as you have the past couple of months."

"It's just a beautiful sight, who wouldn't smile?" I switch the tv monitor to our website when she gets closer to the door. I walk around my desk to greet her. I wrap my arms around her and take in her smell. She smells like heaven to me. "I didn't know you were coming today."

"I was in the area and I thought maybe you would like to take a break and grab some lunch. Hey Mr. Aspen. You guys have the office looking good. Pretty soon business will be rolling in non-stop."

Aspen looks over at me, I just nod my head. I didn't exactly go into details with Journi about what it is we really do, how we do it or how long we've been doing it. I told her we have a business, and this is our first real office. "I'm sure we'll be okay." I walk back around the desk to my seat and Journi takes the seat next to Aspen.

"How are you and Bella?"

"I think you know her a little better than me. You tell me how we're doing."

Shaking her head. "My sister, never makes anything easy."

"That she doesn't. It's nothing I can't handle. That is if I really wanted to handle it."

"Damn, you sound just like her. Alpha male and alpha female. I'll give you a little advice. She's competitive as hell, you'll never win if you keep challenging her. She'll fight you to the very end. Both of you will exhaust yourselves that way. From what she's told me about you, you're very smart. That means you need to outthink her. Beat her at her own game. Push her out of that little comfort zone she's created for herself." Journi was motioning with her hands. The look in Aspen's eyes lets me know he knows exactly what she's talking about.

"She is competitive as fuck. But I get what you saying. I think I know exactly what to do."

"You know what, we should do a cookout. Mecca can you grill?" She didn't wait for me to answer. "That's it, that's what we will do. You come over and invite Legend. It'll be fun."

"Cool, I'll come over. I got some work to do. Bring me something back Mecca."

"You better call Uber eats or something. I'm not sharing what I'm eating." I put an extra emphasis on eating. Journi's head pops around, looking at me like she wants to kill me. Aspen shakes his head and walks out.

"Mecca?"

"Don't be fussing. Come over here and sit on my lap." She comes over and I can't help kissing her. When I finally let her up for air, she's all smiles. "You know you don't need an excuse to come and see me. You're welcome anytime. What's on your mind?" Journi wears her feelings on her face. If she's upset, it shows. She attempts to hide it, but it shows.

"What's on my mind is why Aspen has that lab coat on. I thought this was a security firm."

She laughs and I admire her for a minute. I'm a lucky man to have her in my life. I run my fingers up and down her thighs. She could be the poster girl for thick thighs. "Aspen is extra as fuck. He always doing the most. He builds most of our systems, he calls them his creations. You know like a mad scientist."

"Him and Bella are perfect for each other. They both extra as hell."

"Do I want to know about it?"

"I'll say this Bella likes to play dress up too!"

She laughs like it's the funniest thing in the world. I decide I'll leave it alone. "You still didn't answer my question. What's on your mind beautiful?"

"Well." She stands and walks around to the other side of my desk. "I came over because this school thing may not work out after all. I've come up with a back-up plan. Karm was showing me a few dance studios. It's something I dreamed of, but I planned it for much later in my life. Under the circumstances I think this is the perfect time."

It was the way she said circumstances and avoided eye contact with me. It's her ex again. "Are you excited about it? You seem unsure?"

"It's a big thing. It may seem only like a silly little dance but it's a big thing."

I stand and walk over to her. "There's nothing silly about it. Dance is your passion. I've seen you move and baby girl you brought out passion in me. When you talk about the kids you used to teach, there's this sparkle in your eyes. You take that passion and that sparkle, and you'll build something beautiful. I believe in you."

"Mecca, it means the world to me that you believe in me."

"I want you to believe in yourself. And stop letting people downgrade your dreams."

"Thank you. Thank you for bringing this joy into my life."

"Let's discuss this more over some food. What do you have a taste for today?"

"There's some food trucks over in Colony Square let's see what they have."

"Sounds good to me." She turns and knocks a paper off my desk.

"I see you're thinking about advertising the business. This is a good agency."

She lowers her eyes and takes a deep breath. "They're good but what?"

"My ex works there. I went to a lot of company events with him. It's funny because my sisters joked that I was arm candy just for him to close some of his deals."

I put the paper there to see if she would tell me that he works there. Not that I don't trust her. She holds back when speaking on him. I did my research on him and found all his dirty little secrets. I just want to know how much she knows. I'm waiting on her to trust me enough to tell me. "You're beautiful, smart, cultured and talented. I would take you with me to close any deal. But I'm a jealous man. I wouldn't want anybody looking at you the way I look at you."

"Jealous? Don't tell me once I'm yours you'll get all possessive and shit."

"What do you mean once?" I give her a look and she smiles. I've already laid claim to her. She doesn't understand the power she has over me and how I feel about her. When I peeped her fussing with her ex that day, I had to sit in the car for a minute to cool down. I almost spazzed out on him when I saw him put his hands on her. I had to maintain control. I wasn't ready for Journi to see that side of me. "Let's get out of here and eat. I want to come back and have dessert."

"We can just eat dessert there."

"I want mine in private, full spread eagle on this desk." She licks her lips, gives me a seductive look and starts walking out the door.

I watch her walk away, and those hips put me in trace.

She looks back. "Don't just stand there, let's go. I got some dick waiting on me from the new boss of this fabulous building."

"Correction, CEO, baby! We own this shit."

Chapter 14

Stop Fighting Love

Journi

Alexa play . . . Beyonce. . .Before I Let Go

"Who had this idea to grill out today?"

Bella is eyeing me but I'm not saying nothing, I simply smile. "What?" I can see Karm approaching from the side.

"Yeah, Journi. Got us in here cooking and slaving on this beautiful Saturday."

I walk over to the patio door and motion for them to join. "That right there is the reason." I point at Mecca who was standing at our grill flipping meat like this is his own back yard. This is him in everything he does. When we enter a room together his presence takes over. At first it was a little intimidating to me. A man who speaks power with just his presence. A man who didn't have to say word because it was all in his body language. No matter how much power he would put out he would pull me next to him to make sure I was sharing it with him. I think I admire that the most about him. Whatever he was doing he was including me. He wasn't using me to advance himself. I wasn't his arm piece. I was simply riding with him. And with that body, that mind, that everything, I would ride anywhere with him.

"That's not fair at all. No one wants to lust over that fine specimen of a man in the yard. Looking fine as fuck."

I give Bella a look. "I'm allowing you to look."

Karm gives us both the stink face. "I don't want to look at nothing that belongs to you. All I know is he better know how to grill. I'm famished."

"You've been eating a lot lately. Why don't you ladies invite some people over that you want to look at." I look at them and smile. "I have some friends coming over. I'm about to mix up this punch and it will be a party."

"A party huh? Your ass is up to something. You are not slick Journi." Bella is pointing her finger at me.

"It's just a party. Turn the music up and let me get my boo some water. He looks hot. I mean thirsty." I grab a bottle of water and walk out the patio door. "You look like you really know what you're doing on this grill."

"Beautiful, don't doubt my skills. I'm a master chef on here. Tell me how the match making is going."

"They're suspicious, but they never turn down a party. They'll invite some people over."

"Legend is on his way. I told him to text me when he gets here. This yard is nice. Is this Bella's house?"

"It belongs to all of us. It was for our mom. She left it to us in her will. Karm actually owns the house next door, but she rents it out. Bella is working on getting the house on the other side and I'll take over this one. That way we each have our own but we're still together. I guess it's strange that we enjoy being close to each other."

"Not at all. It's good to see smart, strong sisters that care for and love each other. You ladies are about business." He glances at his phone. "Legend is here. I need to go and assist him with the stuff he brought."

"He didn't need to bring anything. Just himself."

"I think he has something special planned."

I walk to the gate and out to the front with Mecca. Legend is unpacking all kinds of stuff out his car. It looks like he brought everything including his on pot. "Legend, what is all of this?"

"I know y'all from New Orleans. Eating crawfish is like drinking water out there. I figure we could boil a few. I got some crawfish, crab legs, potatoes and some corn."

"We don't have a pot to boil all that stuff in." Mecca walks pass me carrying a huge pot.

Legend pops pass me yelling. "Don't worry I got everything covered."

Legend and Mecca get busy setting everything up. I walk inside and Karm is standing there giving me evil eyes. If looks could kill, I'd be dead. "Is there something wrong Karm?" I know exactly what's wrong. She had been walking around the house moping since the date she had with Legend. Karm was terrified of opening up to someone like Legend. After looking at the glow on her the night she came back in the house, she needs him in her life.

"See I knew your ass was up to something. Why is he here Journi?"

"He's here because him and Mecca are friends." I was trying to play it cool. "I told him to invite some of his friends. I want him to feel comfortable. Some of my friends are on the way. Again, it's a party, Karm." Her eyes get big.

"What friends? Not them heifers from your old job?"

"Well Karm, they are my friends." I purposely invited my thirsty girlfriends. You know the ones that want a man, that will do anything for a man. I know Karm, she's just as competitive as Bella. She will not let anybody sit up and entertain Legend right in front her face. She talking all this mess about him being ghetto and stuff, but she likes it. "Did you invite anyone over? You know some of your friends."

"I know what you're doing, little miss missy. Two can play at this."

"I don't know what you're talking about. But let me go ahead and get these lemons for Legend. He brought everything but the lemons. I told him he's going to need those lemons."

"Lemons? What kind of ghetto drink is he out there trying to make?"

"Girl he's not making no drinks. He's out there about to boil some crawfish, crab legs, potatoes and corn. Talking about he been craving them since New Orleans. I told him I know how it feels. I miss it too!" The look on her face is priceless. She walks over to the patio door. "Yeah, he brought over everything he's going to need. I sure hope he knows what he's doing."

Bella walks up next to her. "Karm, how does he know you love crawfish and crab legs?"

Bingo! Karm loves seafood. She will do anything for it. "Wait Bella you're right that is Karm's favorite food. Bella did you tell him that?"

"You two can kiss my ass. Again, you not slick Journi. I got this."

I don't know if she was saying that to us or herself. But she takes off upstairs with her phone in hand. Before I could say anything, Bella turns and stares me down. "What?"

"All I know is Aspen better not pop-up."

The doorbell rings. "I'll get it." I turn and walk away as quickly as possible. She'll just have to wait and see.

The Barbecue, seafood boil was in full effect. The music was good, the drinks were flowing, and my baby did his thing on that grill. Sitting on his lap showing him how to eat crawfish, I catch a glimpse of Legend. When I say the ladies have loved him all night. They have loved him. Bringing him food or drinks. Laughing at all his jokes. He wasn't even paying them any attention. His eyes were locked on Karm. Karm, who decided to change into some white rip shorts that barely covers her check and a half top that's barely covering her breast. She was sitting between the legs of some guy I've never seen before. He had to be someone she works with because he rolled through here with his nose stuck up in the air at us. However, just like Legend, she wasn't focused on her date. She was focused on Legend. Sneaking a look whenever she got chance.

"What are you looking at?"

"I'm watching Karm and Legend pretend like they aren't looking at each other. It's crazy, why are they fighting it?"

"We can see it. They just have to see it. She's scared of getting hurt and he's not sure if he's ready to knock that wall down."

"I just want her to be happy."

"What I need to know is, am I making you happy?"

I can't help but blush. "Yes." Before I could say another word, I see Aspen walking in with a beautiful woman on his arm. I search for Bella. She hasn't seen him yet. "Mecca, you want some popcorn. The real action is about to start right now. Look who just walked in."

"Why the hell he bringing someone here with him?"

"It's complicated. Just know he's playing the right game."

"Is there something about your sister I don't know?"

"There's a lot about Bella, you and I will never know. She has her secrets. But I'm sure we all do. Just know he's been a part of her world and he's accepting of who she is and how she is."

"What secrets do you have?"

"You'll never know. It wouldn't be a secret if everyone knew."

"I'm not everyone. I'm yours and you belong to me."

The way he said it sent chills up my spine. I've had men that placed claim on me before but none of them were like Mecca. Mecca is demanding without being pushy. It's the way his actions back up his words that makes me feel secure with him. I don't question my place in his heart. I do question my place in his life. There's this air of mystery about him that keeps me questioning am I falling too fast. I tend to do that. Fall for what feels good and looks good. I won't do that to myself again. If I'm jumping, I want to know exactly what I'm jumping into. I didn't realize I was hanging my head until I feel his fingers gently touch my face and pull me in for a kiss.

"If you're not ready, I'll wait for you."

"It's not that. Mecca, this is moving fast."

"Does that scare you?" I watch those gray eyes of his scan me like he was trying to catch a glimpse of my soul.

"I'm terrified that everything about you seems perfect. I'm scared that the things I don't know about you will come back and bite me in the ass. I'm fearful you're going to hurt me. Especially when you realize I'm not everything you've built me up to be." I've been playing poker with Mecca. But I just laid out all my cards. It was time for him to know why I was holding back.

"I'm not perfect. Far from it. I have a past. As we both do. I can't judge you on yours. Just like I wouldn't want you judging me on mine. My background is not super clean, but it made me into the man I am today. I would never intentionally do anything to hurt you. I want to protect that heart of yours. I completely understand your fears after everything you've been through. I can sit here and tell you a million things, that will sound good. I won't. I'd rather show and prove who I am to you. I'll let my actions speak for themselves. I told you before, I see you for who you are, and I meant it."

I hear everything he's saying. The thing about the past and secrets is they have a way of reappearing. Maybe I wasn't afraid of his secrets but terrified he would find out mine. I wrap my arms around his neck and relax. If this doesn't work, I at least want to remember how good he makes me feel.

Chapter 15

A Magnetic Pull

Karman

Alexa play . . . Jeremih and Ne-Yo. . .U 2 Luv

If Chad could stop moving his big ass head, I could get a better view of Legend. I don't even know why I invited him. Oh, I know why, it was a last, minute thing. Chad has been trying to get me to go on a date with him for the past few months. I met him at the Starbucks one day while I was getting my coffee fix. He's an investment banker that's extremely easy on the eyes. We've only spoken on the phone a few times since that day. After the first conversation, I knew he wasn't my type. However, in my line of business networking and connections are everything. I made sure to keep our lines of communications open. I had to think of someone to call at the last minute. He answered and was excited to come and hang out. Now I'm regretting it because his ass just can't shut up.

He moves a little to the left laughing at some corny joke he just told, I finally get a clear view of Legend. I swear Journi's thirsty ass friends have been all up in his face since they walked in here. He's been eating it up with his loud ass. Laughing and smiling and dancing with them. He's standing over there smiling in a trick's face and she's giggling like a bobble head. I like the grill he has in today. Each time he smiles I can see it and I can feel my pussy getting wetter and wetter. His attire today is casual. He's wearing a Kobe Bryant jersey and a Laker's basketball short set. I want to say he looks crazy in it. But that would be a lie. He looks down-right sexy in it. His whole body is perfect. My eyes fall on that damn print and

I almost start salivating. I don't know what's wrong with me. I focus back on Chad. "I'm glad you were able to come today."

"Me too. I got to say you're a little different than I thought. I mean way different."

It's the way he said different. Different like it was the worst thing in the world. "Different how?"

"You're so very professional all the time. I appreciate that in you because I like your work ethic. It matches mine. I just didn't expect the tattoos. You must have gotten those in your younger days. I know a doctor that can remove those for you. You shouldn't have to look at your past now that you've gotten your life together and you have this bright future ahead of you."

All I could do was look at him. I can't believe this pampered, manicured hands fool didn't just dismiss my tattoos like they're nothing. "How about another drink?" I get up and walk away before he could even answer. Its men like him that make me feel like I'll never find the right man. Men in the streets understand me and I understand them. Men with degrees want to change me into the perfect little homemaker. Why can't I have the in between?

I pass by Legend not even making eye contact with him. Clearly, he's found acceptance. Before I could make it into the house, I feel someone tug on the buckle of my shorts. They pull me around and I come face to face with Legend.

"You just gone walk pass me like you didn't see me."

"I saw you. I figured you was busy entertaining."

"This personality is magnetic. I draw people in."

"Shit, does attract flies."

"Damn shorty! That tongue is vicious. I bet it works wonders on the right spot."

As he said that he grabbed himself. I couldn't help but look. I'll admit the vision of me on my knees pleasing him popped into my head. I had to shake that shit off. "Don't be disrespectful."

"I'm just speaking how I feel. Like how I'm feeling these shorts on you. And this top."

He pulls me closer. He glides the tips of his fingers around the outline of my top. My nipples get hard. "I need a drink." The words barely come out. He had me up here stuttering. The way he's eyeing my nipples and licking his lips had me on the verge of exploding.

"While you in there get a plate too. I didn't see you eat any crawfish or crab legs. I fixed it just for you."

Before I could respond. I see Chad approaching. This is not good.

"Karman are you ok. Is this clown bothering you?"

"Clown, nigga who the fuck is you?"

I get in between them. "Chad it's fine. Go sit back down. It's ok."

"No Karman. I saw him putting his hands on you. Making you uncomfortable."

"Please Chad just have a seat."

"Yeah Chad! Have a fucking seat. Before I sit your ass down."

I look around and Journi and Mecca are sitting down like they watching a movie. Bella has her phone out ready to record. Aspen is standing off to the side with a smirk on his face. None of them was about to come and help me. I turn and look Legend right in his eyes. "Legend please. For me." He stands back and relaxes his hands right in front of him.

"Don't beg this clown. He's beneath us. Maybe if you weren't dressed like that, he wouldn't be approaching you that way."

I look at Chad and understand why I wasn't feeling him. He was clueless and hypercritical. If I were to ever give him a chance, he would've tried to change everything about me. "Dressed like what?"

"Come on you know what I mean."

"Your eyes must be broke. Karm is looking sexy as fuck right now. Got my dick all hard and shit."

"You see what I mean Karman. You have to respect yourself first. Or else you get disrespectful little boys approaching you with clown shit like this."

"That's your last time using that clown word. You the court jester. She using you for entertainment. You been in her ear over there all night shooting your shot. But you not even the game."

"Karman tell your sisters to get their guest."

He smirks, like he's about to do something. I already know his type. He won't do nothing. "Maybe, I'm still stuck on the part where you think I'm dressed inappropriately. It's a backyard grill out. How should I be dressed?"

"You're missing the point. You're out displaying those horrid tattoos and all your skin. You're basically asking for it."

Before I could say anything, Legend pushes pass me.

"What's disrespectful is you standing up here taking the anger you have for me out on her. Only a fool would blame his lady. You mad at me say it to me." He walks closer to him. "You CEO wannabe boss type niggas all the same. All talk. What's sad is you don't know beauty when you see. Every picture, every symbol, every word on her frame is walking art. It's stunning and beautiful." He turns and nods his head at me. "But it would take a real man to recognize that shit." He turns again and looks at me. "Send this bitch ass nigga on his way before I do."

He didn't even need to tell me twice. "Umm Chad, you got to go."

"You wasn't worth my time anyway. Ghetto bitch."

Legend runs over to him and hits him with a right hook, he stumbles and falls. Legend picks him up and tosses him out the yard. He shrugs when I gasp. "I was trying for you to keep my hands off of him. But no one disrespects you."

"That's fine and all but what about you."

"What about me?"

"You was stilling over there entertaining them."

"Fuck them thirsty hoes. I can have my pick of any one of them. I don't want them. I want you. You fighting it. But I know you feel me."

He was right. I was feeling the hell out of him. The way he spoke about me. Made me feel so damn good. I date a lot of Chads and I'm one of two things to them, the ghetto experience. Or because I'm successful they are just trying to say they had me. This is true of both white men and black men. They were the same. "Legend, I—"

"You nothing. I came over here and slaved over that hot ass pot to fix your favorite food. I got into it with that wannabe important nigga for you and now you standing here in my face telling me about something that don't even matter."

He walks up to me and places his fingers in the slits of my jeans and rips it more in two spots. I start thinking about the night we spent together above the city. I can't help the way I'm drawn to him.

"Go over there fix your ass a damn plate and come sit outside and talk to me. Tell me how I did too because I know I made it good."

All I could say was. "Ok."

He gets closer and whispers in my ear. "After you eat. I'm taking you upstairs and fucking all that *you don't wanna be with me* out of you."

He walks behind me and taps me on ass. I take my crazy butt over and start fixing my plate. Journi comes in and starts pretending like she fixing herself a plate. I just look at her.

"Hurry up and fix that plate before he comes back and checks you again." She winks at me and walks away.

Once my plate is done, I walk over by Legend and he motions for me to come and sit between his legs. I sit down and he leans over my shoulder.

"I put my foot in that shit. It's going to be good."

Fifteen minutes later he and I was up in my room. He was working my body like it was a job. It was sweet, ruff, nasty sex. I was enjoying every single moment. When I feel my body shake, he turns me over and starts grinding to the beat of the song playing outside.

"You hear that, I don't want nobody else. I only want you to love."

When he says love my body tenses up.

"Relax, I'm not proclaiming my love. At least not yet. But you feel this just as much as I feel you."

When he's done working my body, I stretch out on the bed. He lays next to me. I can feel his fingers tracing my tattoos. "Thank you for defending me tonight. I know people think tattoos are weird but to me they allow me to express myself when I'm unable to speak."

"I can't imagine you not being able to speak how you feel. But I understand. I love them on you. Don't let these wannabe boss types make you feel insecure about yourself. They out here pretending for the world. They can't understand you, because you're real. You just don't want everyone to see your real side. That's why you keep these hidden. But I see them, but mainly I see you. They're prolific just like you."

"Prolific, look at you with the big words." He gets really quiet. I sit up to make eye contact with him. "It was a joke. I didn't mean it to be offensive. I know you're smart. In fact, you might be one of the smartest I know. I know that from the conversations we've had. I don't think I'm the only one in the room whose hiding pieces of themselves from the world."

"Just know, I won't hide anything from you. Rock with me. Give me a chance."

He was asking for me to do the thing I promised I would never do again. I could continue to run from this feeling he gives, or I could run into it. I like being around Legend. He's loud and vulgar and crazy. He's also fun, caring and supportive. He appeals to both sides of me. The way he makes me feel is crazy. "I can't make you any promises. Just like I don't want you making false promises to me. I like this feeling. I like you. Let's just see where this goes."

Chapter 16

Do I Seem Like the Type to Ask Why Her?

Bella

Alex play. . . Jazmine Sullivan. . . Forever Don't Last

Sitting back, laughing at how Karman just had her ass given to her was comical to me. No one, well besides me, has put Karm in her place in a minute. Legend had her eating out of his hand. When I see them two go in the house, I know they won't be back out tonight. Whatever he's about to lay on her is well needed. She always has her panties in a bunch about something. She doesn't allow herself to relax. All she focuses on is work, Journi and me. More Journi than me. But we both focus on her. Journi, being the youngest, we always want to protect her. Even though we know full well, she can handle herself. Journi, seems helpless and innocent but she's far from it. I glance at her sitting with Mecca. They make a cute couple. He's good for her because he caters to the side of her that Bayden was trying to erase. Bayden was a fucking joke. He hurt Journi more times than I could count. I don't know why she stayed with him for long. I'm all for forgiving your man, but my sister was acting like she was auditioning for an episode of For My Man. If he said jump, she said how high. He cheated on her numerous times. When she came to the hospital last year with a STD that was creating pain in her pelvic, we found out she was pregnant. She thought a baby would make him change his ways. Make him finally commit to her. Two days later, I was sitting with her at an abortion clinic holding her hand. He told her; it just wasn't the right time to start a family. I wanted to kick his ass. If Karm would have known she would have wanted to kick his ass too! Journi made me promise to not tell her. At the time mom was getting sicker and we didn't need to worry her anymore. I don't think she would have told me, but she needed me to come with her. He went out of town on one of his work adventures, coincidently that day. I watched the sparkle fade from my sister's eyes that day. Tonight, I can see it coming back.

"I see your man brought a new dish for you tonight. He must be sick of me."

I look over at Shay and I want to slap her. "He's not my man."

"Denial huh?"

"Not denial. We're not in a relationship. We're just kicking it."

"If you say so. She's fine. I wouldn't mind doing her."

I'd been evading looking in Aspen's direction. I saw him when he first walked in with that heifer on his arm. I told him before, I bring the girls. And here he is bringing her up in here like it's a gift for me. She's beautiful, I'll admit it. And fine as fuck just like Shay said, but she wasn't my type. "She's not my type."

"Your type is the girl of your own choosing. Whenever I pick out a girl you always turn them down. If you had saw her first, you would have picked her."

Shay is wrong. I don't do that. Do I? Well maybe. But it's my choice, my rules and my way. Except Aspen wasn't the type to keep letting me have it my way. For the past few weeks, he's been pressing me about going to dinner. Maybe a movie. He even tried to take me to a concert at the City Winery. I would ask could Shay come or invite another friend and he would say, just us tonight. Since that first night with me, him and Shay, we've seen each other only two more times. I figured he enjoyed it. But I noticed he was way more attentive to me than Shay. He would please her at my request only. It was getting a little weird because he started acting like she wasn't in the room. Like I said before Shay and I are friends. I would never want to hurt her feelings.

"Bella, let me be real with you. That man is feeling you. He got to enjoy the fantasy of having two beautiful women. It's old to him."

"It's not old to me."

"That's because you're using threesomes like a crutch. Truth is you're using me like a crutch. I'm your fall back. I make you feel secure in this world that you've created for yourself. In your world, there's no chance of falling for anyone, which means no chance of getting hurt. We all play by your rules because your rules give you control over everything. He's not the type to keep following your rules. He's a real man. He's looking for more than a quick nut in the bedroom."

"That's just it, I don't want more."

"Please you've been booted up since he walked in. And before he came you were checking your phone like crazy. I'm sure you were waiting on a text from him. Your mouth can say a lot of things Bella, but I know you."

"Then you know me well enough to know I can let it go with no problem."

"I know you can. But I like him for you."

"You mean for us." She sits up in her chair.

"We're not in a relationship. I'm just someone you do. You're comfortable with me. But that's it. Besides, as hard as this is for me to say, I've met someone."

I couldn't believe my ears. As much as I didn't want to accept it, she was right. She and I are friends. She's not my girlfriend. It just feels good to have someone around that I completely trust. A person I know that's not out to hurt me. I can't picture my world not having her in it. "What about us?"

"I will always be your friend. But that's it. I really like this guy and I want to give him all of me. Not just pieces of me."

"Do I know him?"

"No. I've told him about me, but he's not open to this world. And that's okay with me because I'm ready to close the door to this world. I'm ready and open to a new adventure. Besides, if he would have gotten a taste of you, he would've been walking away from me."

"You know that's not true. You're irresistible. You're a wonderful person inside and out and anyone is lucky to have you." Shay is a great lover, but she's also a phenomenal person and awesome friend. I'm going to miss her. But I understand. "You're just selfish. Found your ass some good dick and didn't want to share it with me." We both laugh. I can't be mad at her. Shay, like me was fighting falling in love again. If she found someone worth her time, I'm going to be the biggest cheerleader in her quest for love. I bring her in for a hug. "I'm happy for you. I wish you nothing but the best. If you need me, I'm a phone call away."

"Thank you. I got to go he made plans for us tonight. Bella, don't have regrets in life. Broken hearts mend. Give him a chance."

She gets up and walks away. Sadness falls on me like a ton of bricks. What was I going to do now? The club won't be the same without her. Could I be the same without her?

"Are you okay?"

His voice knocks me out of my zone. It also sends a chill up my spine. I need him right now. I need him to hold me and tell me that it'll be okay. But I can't say that to him. "I'm good, why?" I look up and our eyes meet. I look away as quickly.

"Why did Shay leave? I was making my way over to speak to her."

"Just to her?"

"She was the only one who waived when I walked in here. You were over here rolling them beautiful eyes."

And I was. "You walk in here with build a barbie. And you want me all in your face. She's not my type by the way."

"She's not into women. She's on a strict dick diet."

"She ain't me though."

"Exactly."

I almost break my neck, looking back at his ass. "You said that like something is wrong with me?"

"That's up for debate."

"Aspen, don't play with me. What the fuck does that mean? You said you wouldn't judge me on what I like."

"You got it twisted. I'll never judge you on your fetishes. I'm willing to accept all of you. The unfortunate thing is you won't let me know any other parts of you. You show me the insecure side that hides behind other people."

"I'm not insecure. Far from it."

"Not insecure the way you think. Insecure in showing who you really are to me and to the world. Listen, I'm not going to try and explain something you already know."

He was wrong, I'm not insecure. I'm not hiding behind anyone. I'm just not ready to have my heart broken into pieces all over again. "It's not like you think. I'm not like you think."

"I think you're afraid of being alone with me. We can't even have a normal date Bella."

"Maybe your normal is not my normal."

"What the does even mean? Just admit you have a wall up and you're afraid to let me in."

I wasn't going to admit anything. No matter how intently he was looking at me hoping I would answer him. His eyes are pleading with me. I want to say exactly how I feel. I want to say how much I want him to get to know me. To understand me. To know all my dark secrets. I want to say how much I want him to be in my life. But the words are escaping me. I just can't bring myself to say them. "I'm not afraid of anything." His eyes switch from the warmest eyes to ice cold.

"Fine. I have a date; I don't want to be rude and leave her by herself all night."

"Aspen."

"No, Bella, I'm not playing this game with you. Either you want to be with me, or you don't. Either you're letting me in, or you won't. But you won't keep playing with me."

When I don't say anything, he brings his hands to my cheeks and pulls me close to him. He kisses me on the forehead. When he turns and walks away, I feel a coldness creep into my body. I was let go twice tonight. But this one feels like a gut kick. It feels like I can't catch my breath. I watch him grab build-a-barbie and walk out the yard. I can't move, I feel like I'm frozen in place. I'm just standing here attempting to make myself move. I feel arms wrap around my waist.

"Are you okay?"

I snatch her hands from around me with a quickness. "Really Journi? You walk your happy ass over here to gloat. You think this is a game. It's not. This is my life. You're walking around here trying to play match maker. When you can't even handle your own love life. Tell that man the truth. Tell him that if Bayden walks in here today or tomorrow your crazy ass would take him right back. You enjoyed the abuse that nigga gave you. You enjoyed being his arm-candy that he pushed around. You got off on being his toy and prop for his back room deals. Tell him how you crave that sickness. Because to you the sickness was a cure. Wait until the innocence you like to display starts to wear thin and he sees you for who you really are." I leave her standing there speechless. She thought she was doing something. She was only fucking up my life. I will not be forced to be something I'm not.

I refuse to be that girl. I refuse to ask him why he picked her over me. I refuse to lay all my cards down and let him play me. I refuse to be someone's puppet like her. Falling for man after man. Never stepping back and allowing herself to heal.

I don't regret anything I've said. It's true. If Bayden walks in here tonight she would run right into his arms. That is if she hasn't already made plans to go back and be with him. It doesn't matter how nice Mecca is to her. She prefers the man that treats her like shit. She can say whatever she wants about my dark side. I'm upfront with mine. Unlike her. She thinks I don't know the other ways he used her to climb his way to the top. Sooner or later she'll need to let out her dark too. I just hope Mecca can handle it.

Chapter 17

Losing What I Thought I Knew

Mecca

Alexa play. . . Jay-Z. . .Lost One

If I say Journi and I are in a strange place that would be an understatement. It felt like we were on a fast track to a happy life. I'll be the first to admit I fell for Journi hard and fast. That night I saw her at the club, I saw both her good and bad side. A bad side she likes to tuck in like it's a blouse and she has to keep it neatly tucked in her pants at all times. The bad side that she let loose in the bedroom when she wasn't worried about being perfect. A bad side that attracts me more than anything to her. I heard her sister loud and clear that night. It wasn't the bad side that was pushing me away from her. It was the possibility of her being in contact with her ex. I did something I don't usually do; I pulled her cell phone records. She was talking or texting him daily. When I saw that I knew why she continued to hold back from me. She wasn't done with her past relationship. Each time she called me I told her I was busy with work. Truth was I was giving her space to figure things out. Yes, I want her. Yes, I care for her. But I won't be the rebound man. She's either with me because she wants me and feels the same way I feel. But there won't be an in between.

In the meantime, while she was figuring out her situation, I was working on a situation that needs a resolution. I looked into Swiss like Legend asked me to do. Everything that I pulled up was bad.

"Hey, I got that system ready for install. I want to do a quick run through. I need to make sure there are no blind spots."

I look up and Aspen is standing in the door of my office. "Cool, I'll come with you to check it out."

"No hot lunch date today?"

A smile spreads across my face. "Not today. I'm giving her a little space."

"You know all that shit you said Bella said was probably just talk. She was angry at me. And she just took it out on her."

"I knew that when she said it. But she was right about Journi still talking with her ex. She needs a minute to figure some things out."

"Did she say that, or did you make decision for her?"

"I just made it easy for her."

"Don't let that nigga walk back into her life and erase your ass."

That would never happen. Once a voyage to Mecca has been taken nothing else feels the same. "Don't worry about it. I know what I'm doing." I slide the file that I was holding across my desk to Aspen. "It's not good." Aspen opens it and starts glancing over all the information.

"I never trusted his ass. Even back in the day he was a snake. But this right here is low even for him."

"Legend should be here any minute."

"He's going to flip out and kill him."

"I know that's why I wanted him to come here. We can at least try and talk him down."

"I got something that might hold him."

Aspen darts out the office and comes back with some straps. "What the hell is that?"

"It'll hold his crazy ass down."

I look closer at it and I realize what it is. "Aspen, your ass is wild. First, I find out Bella got your ass doing threesomes and now you traveling with sex toys. You a wild boy."

"I ain't traveling with nothing. I had it in my bag. You know just in case Bella calls; I want to be prepared. She wasn't my first threesome. She just does them better than any women I've meet."

All I could do was look at him and fall out laughing. "Man, she done turned your ass out."

"I think they got voodoo in their pussies. Got all of us hooked on them and doing strange shit."

"Go put that shit up. I ain't using that on no man. You crazy." I can't stop laughing. Aspen, was serious about trying to use that damn thing.

"You right he might rip my shit before I get to use it."

"Man, I'll just have some of the crew on stand-by." Still laughing, I get an alert from security that Legend has arrived. I tell them to bring him on up. "Get ready he's here." In true Legend form he walks through the office talking loud and crazy.

"Look at this shit right here. Man, this is money right here. Let me get a job. Hire my ass. I need this kind of money in my life."

We have a few employees in the office now and they were all just looking at him. "Bring your loud ass on in here making all that noise disturbing our staff."

"Yes, sir boss. I don't want to get fired before I'm hired."

He walks in daps me and Aspen and continues to whistle while walking around my office. "I'm glad you could come in today."

"Listen, before we get down to business, this is nice. Two knuckle heads from NY did all of this right here. I knew business was booming but not like this booming. This is nice. I'm proud of you both."

"See I told you Mecca. It's Voodoo in the pussy. His ass under some kind of spell. Coming in here giving us compliments and being all nice. It's Voodoo!"

Legend looks at me. "He's convinced Journi, Bella and Karman have done some damn Voodoo on us."

"Shit, if they have, I like it. I'm all ready to change my religion and get some goats or chickens to sacrifice. Karm is my baby. I'll paint my face and run around in circles chanting if she asks me to do it."

"Right there, proves my point. They have Voodoo in their pussies."

"Whatever they got; it's not changing the craziness in both of your asses." Aspen closes the door. I motion for Legend to take a seat. "I followed-up on what we talked about concerning Swiss. It's not good. Before I show you everything, I need you to remember how nice you think this office is and don't be in here fucking our shit up. Or else Aspen will strap you up in a sex toy." The look on Legend's face is priceless. I fall out laughing all over again. He looks at Aspen.

"What kind of kinky shit you into now?"

"I'll teach you later." Aspen takes a seat on the side of my desk and smirks.

"When you said Swiss was moving funny, that was a lie. He's not moving funny. He's moving with complete purpose." Legend looks through the folder in front of him. It takes a minute for everything to hit him. He looks back at me, only this time, his eyes aren't friendly. They're black as night. Legend is colorful, loud and fun but he's also a coldhearted, ruthless savage in the streets. He's responsible for the death of more than I can name or even care to count. Don't let his sense of humor fool you. He'll carve up your face and slit your throat all while making a joke and laughing.

"How long?"

"All the information I pulled has checks cashed by him for the past five years. I also checked his bank accounts and I show large deposits going back even further. We don't know everything they know but we know they know something." Legend throws the papers across the room.

"If he's been feeding them information that long. They know almost everything about how I run my operation. And everything about me."

He stands, throws everything on the floor, picks up a chair and throws it full force breaking the glass wall of my office. I see our crew getting our employees to exit the floor. Him and Swiss have been operating as brothers for years. They are tight. Thick as thieves together. Up until a few months ago I'm sure Legend considered him a friend. To learn your friend, someone you trusted is living foul is heartbreaking.

Aspen moves my other chair to the side of him. "I hate to state the obvious here but if he's been feeding them information this long, they have a case built up on you, your crew, your connect and possibly us too."

Legend starts walking in a circle. He screams and punches a hole in my wall. "I'll kill him. Kill him with my bare fucking hands."

I see the member of our crew start walking toward the office, I wave my hand to back them down. "Listen don't do anything crazy yet. I have an inside person. Let me get with them first. Get all the facts."

"I don't need any more facts. He knows almost everything about my shit. He knows enough to put me away for life."

Aspen shakes his head. "That's true. The thing that bothers me is why haven't they taken you down? If they have all they need to know why haven't they made a move."

"That's the big question Aspen. We need to find out. We also need to find out if he's working solely with the FBI. We need a plan. Legend you can't touch him." He's completely ignoring me. "We don't know what they know. We can't act until we know what they know."

"Don't tell me what the fuck to do. If I want to kill him, I'll kill him!"

"If this was just about you that would be fine. At this point everyone we know is involved. We need to know exactly what he's told them. We need to find out who's the real target. If we don't, we run the risk of everyone we know going down. That includes Karman, Bella and Journi." Legend stops pacing the floor and looks at me.

"I can't let that happen to my baby. She doesn't deserve that. None of them do."

"Take a seat Legend. We need to come up with a plan. I need to know everything he knows about your operation." Legend takes a long deep breath.

"Aspen was right he knows pretty much everything. Except a few things. I started selling off my territories a few years ago. You know trying to make my exit. I never told him because that's around the time he started moving strange to me. Always on my back about letting him know what my next move was about to be. Why I wouldn't go to war with certain people? He didn't know I had given those territories to the people he wanted me to go to war with."

"That's smart. How deep are you in right now?"

"Deep enough to still be running half of New York. I'm mixed in with Atlanta, New Orleans and Cali."

"That means we need to warn everyone. You need to get with your connect and warn them too."

"Wait, that's the only thing he doesn't know. He doesn't know my connects. He's been on my ass about me introducing him to them. Talking about he thinks we need to branch out. I never took him with me to any of the meetings. I told you about the incident with Fire."

It hits me like a ton of bricks. "That's it! They haven't made a move because they're waiting to bust your connects. For five years they been trying to narrow down your connects. They want to take you down and everyone associated with you. Somebody is trying to make a big name for themselves."

"We just need to figure out who. In the meantime, I'll check all the cameras we have installed at your house. If he's talking to anyone in there, we'll know about it. Mecca, get someone on him and let's get his phone cloned. It's time we know who he's talking with and what he's saying."

"Aspen is right it's time to get ahead of him. I'll get in contact with my contact over at the agency. Legend, until we know everything. We can't make a move on him. We need him alive." He turns away from me, avoiding eye contact. "Legend don't be a hot head on this right now. We all have too much on the line. Just give me and Aspen a few days and we'll find out everything."

"I'll give you your time. But I want everything on him. His family, his blood type, what he eats every day. Everything! I don't care what it cost. Even if you have to get that crazy bitch involved. I'll chill for now, but I can't be around him. If I put eyes on him, I'll kill him." He brushes his clothes off and walks towards the door.

Aspen stands in front of me. "Mecca, your contact is it who I think it is?"

"I can handle it."

"You say that shit now. You just found someone to make you happy. That crazy bitch will smell that happiness on you and try to rip little Journi to pieces. Just let me talk with my people first."

I nod my head as he walks out the door. I wasn't about to let Legend get himself in trouble. He's saved me too many times. I wasn't about to let everything we all worked hard to build fall down. If Legend gets jammed up, we all do. I won't let that happen to any of us. If I had to open my closet and let some skeletons out, then that's what I need to do. I pick up my phone. There's a text from Journi asking me to meet her. She'll have to wait. I hit the number for the person I've been avoiding for years. When she picks up, I can hear the venom in her tone.

"Well, well, well it must be raining problems. I know you only called because something is wrong. Tell me handsome what can I do for you?"

"We need to talk."

"I don't even get a hello first."

"Why bother, you know why I called."

“Damn, just that voice of yours has my pussy purring.”

“Calm down. This is a business matter.”

“Mecca with you, it’s never business, it’s pleasure. All my pleasure. Send me a location and time.”

“The usual place.” I hang up. I feel like I’m opening Pandora’s box. The difference is I already know what’s in the inside. Something dark, devious, and painful. Before I head over to the airport. I need to see her. I need to feel the feeling she brings to me. The calm and heat she gives my body. I need the gentleness of her touch and the fire of the passion she gives. I want to give her space, but I need to prepare her for the storm I can feel brewing.

Chapter 18

Losing All Control

Bella

Alexa play. . .Migual. . . R.A.N

Today, I'm working my fifth, twelve-hour shift in a row. I wouldn't even use the word exhausted to describe me. I would say dead on my feet but since they are killing me, they're reminding me that I'm still alive. Usually, I don't work this many shifts in a row but sitting at home was driving me crazy. It's driving me crazy for a few reasons. One, Journi's ass is still upset with me. She blames me because Mecca hasn't been around lately. Two, Karm has been on my ass about apologizing. And three, when everything around me is still and quiet, thoughts of Aspen invade my space like a room filled with smoke. Am I sorry for the things I said and did? Just a little. I didn't mean to hurt Journi. I know she truly likes Mecca. He's one of the best things that's happened in her life in a minute. The fact still remains, she has to be honest with him. I know she's still been in contact with Bayden. I know because I saw her responding to his text and talking with him on the phone. I love my sister, but the girl loves pain. I don't care how many times he's hurt her she runs back to him like he has something on her that keeps her at his side. I'm not about to let Karm boss me into apologizing. I only spoke the truth.

Am I sorry about Aspen? At first, I wasn't. No one told him to catch feelings. I told him upfront what this was. He's just fun, a toy to me. We have fun together. Why can't a woman just enjoy being sexually free? I like deciding. I like not being dedicated to one person. I like being alone. At least, I used to like being alone.

Something feels like it's changed. I've spoken with Shay a few times. She's so happy it's almost contagious. Going to the club and not seeing her there was killing me. She has been my fall back plan for a while now. I wasn't that for her. She deserved more than me using her for my pleasure. She confessed to me how happy she was that I had found someone to fill the empty space in me, just like she found the same thing. I didn't have the heart to tell her Aspen and I weren't together. I didn't want her to worry about me. She's been a great friend to me. I've been the one holding her back. I've been the one requiring her to be here at my every beck and call. Requiring her to accept whatever mood I was in for the night. She never complained, she simply went along. I honestly thought It would be her and I that ended up together. But she was honest with me about wanting a family and kids. She said she just didn't want to end up married and ten years or twenty years later regret not allowing herself to explore her sexual fantasies. I had to laugh at that one. She can die a happy one. Believe me there was not one fantasy she didn't get to explore and live out.

My plan tonight is a long hot bath and climbing in bed to sleep until my body says I've had enough. I have to check on a few more patients, one more hour and I'm done. I get to a room that has a light on. Someone may have left it on by mistake. It should be empty, but I notice someone laying in the bed. I walk in to grab the chart. As head nurse I know everything going on, on my floor. If someone has messed up and put a patient on my floor I'm going off. I don't need any fuck ups today. Today was about me coasting through my shift and getting out of here without the drama today. "Hello, I'm nurse Fields, I'm going to take a look at your chart. How are you today?" Before I could reach the chart, someone walks out the bathroom, slams the door and stands there guarding it. The person lying in bed pulls the cover back and hops out the bed. He's fully dressed, shoes and all.

"You know you're fine as fuck. I mean in your clothes you look good. But that uniform makes you look even finer. It must be custom made because it's fitting your body like a glove. Chocolate and beautiful. What a combination."

I back up. "What do you want?"

"I just want to talk."

"What do we need to talk about? And why like this? Blocking the door and all dramatic and shit."

"All that sassiness with no fear. I would like that under different circumstances."

He walks closer to me, circling my body, examining me from head to toe. "Say what you need to say and let me out this room."

"As much as they say you like foreplay, I thought we would have a little fun first."

His words sent a chill down my spine. How did he know me? I've never seen him in my life before.

"Don't worry your secrets are safe with me. I won't tell anyone at your job how you like to play in your spare time. What I may do is stop by that exclusive club and see if I can take you for a ride."

"You wish. Get to the fucking point." He backs up and holds his hands up in a surrender motion.

"I guess you need to be in the club to relax enough for me. But let me get right to it. You and I have some friends in common. Basically, I need you to get a message to our friends. I know they living foul. I need them to know, that I know. If any other members of my crew gets busted or God forbid, I get busted." He put his hands up to touch me. He runs his fingers down my face and stops at my breast. “Let him know, I promise you’ll look just as beautiful in a body bag.”

He turns to walk toward the door. The guy who was with him, opens the door and leaves first. The other guy turns around and gives me an evil smile.

“Let Aspen and Mecca know, Drill said hello.”

When the door closes, I let out the breath I’ve been holding. I carry a gun, mace and a taser. But not in the hospital. Not while I’m working. My stuff is either in my car or my work locker. If, Drill, as he called himself had walked up on me while I was headed to or in my car, he’d be dead. His ass would be speaking to the devil and not Aspen.

I pull out my phone and call Aspen and tell him to meet me somewhere safe. I text both of my sisters and let them know to be on guard. I tell them I’ll explain it when I see them. I work the rest of my shift as if nothing happened. At the end of my shift, I make it to my locker. I pull out my mace and taser. I know my gun is in the car. Walking through the parking lot I’m watching my surrounds. I hate to admit it, but I’m scared. Growing up in New Orleans our lives haven’t always been crime free. But we were blessed enough to have cousins, uncles and friends that watched our back. Right now, I don’t have those people surrounding me. I know if I call them it would be an all-out war in Atlanta. My sisters and I live a certain lifestyle out here. My mother made sure we were in a different world and different environment. I guess forever don’t last always. Hitting the unlock button on my car, someone puts a hand on my shoulder. I turn around ready to mace whomever it is.

“Hold up shorty be careful where you point that thing.”

"Dammit Aspen! Why the hell would you sneak up on me like that?"

"Your voice on the voicemail you left me, worried me."

"That doesn't mean come creeping up on me in the middle of the night in an empty parking lot."

"What's wrong? You're shaking."

The welcoming smile he was wearing was replaced with a serious look. He put his hands over mine. The warmness of them sent a volt of relief shooting through me. I feel safe. I shouldn't feel safe. We are standing outside in the middle of a parking lot and anyone can see us. Anything could happen to us. Looking into Aspen's eyes made me feel like everything was okay. I honestly didn't think he would respond to the message I left for him. I know how angry he was with me. I know how we left things the last time I saw him. But he's right here. That made me feel dumb as hell for pushing him out of my life. Aspen is a real man. "A guy cornered me at my job today. Him and another guy. He said to give you and Mecca a message."

"Wait me and Mecca. Did they hurt you?"

He was rubbing his hands through my hair and inspecting my body for damages. "No, but at work I don't carry my protection. I just keep thinking what if."

With a look of concern on his face, he looks around. "Let's go to my car. I'll have someone from my crew come and pick your car up. You can't drive like this and I'll feel better with you next to me."

Shit, I feel better too! But I wasn't about to say it to him. I just nodded my head and went in the direction he was guiding my body to go. I wasn't going to fight him tonight. I wasn't going to say to him I could protect myself. The only thing I would do is allow him to lead tonight. When we got in his car, I sat back and relaxed. He takes my hand and drives.

We end up at his office. I don't understand why we're there, but I didn't question it either. I follow him in the building, to my surprise there are workers there and it seems like normal business is going on. It's the middle of the night. "It's after hours."

"We're security. We make sure clients are safe day in and day out. Come on we can talk in my office."

To say I'm impressed with the layout of Aspen's office is an understatement. His office is huge. His office is decorated in a modern black and white design. What stands out the most are the degrees hanging on the walls. I know he's smart, but I might need to upgrade that to genius. The walls are covered with all types of accolades. It's true you never judge a book by its cover. Aspen's outside, beautiful and pleasing to the eye. He's a manly man and it shows in everything he does. His sex appeal walks in the room before he does most days. Any woman would be, well is, attracted to him. Aspen's brain and intellect, is a different story. The brilliance on this wall is enough to make you cum without him even touching you. But it screams nerd and some women can't handle a smart ass.

"Bella, you need some water or something stronger to drink?"

"Just some water." He hands me a bottle and I gulp it down right away. My mouth was dry.

"The guys who came at you tonight. What did they say?"

"They were going on and on about you and Mecca ratting on them. And he said if he got busted, he would put me in a body bag. And—" I didn't realize I was shaking again until he put his hands on my shoulder to stop me.

“Calm down Bella. Drink some more water. Tell me what they looked like.”

“The one who did the most talking, he said his name was Drill. He was tall and muscled like Shug Knight.” The look on Aspen’s face changed from relaxed to something I hadn’t seen before on him. It was the look of a pure monster.

“Did you say Drill?”

“Yeah, he said Drill.”

“Did he touch you Bella? Tell me the fucking truth. I will kill him if he was even breathing wrong on you.”

“He only scared me. I’m okay. I promise. I’m good.” He starts pacing the floor. Now he was scaring me. The whole time I’ve known him. He’s been the fun, easy going guy. I’ve never seen him angry. Never seen him like this. There’s a knock at his office door. It makes me jump.

“Come in.”

My sisters walk in with Legend right behind them. They run up to me and hug me. When they release me, I watch Aspen motion for Legend to leave with him out the door.

I take a minute and explain what happened to them. “This can’t be good. I mean just the look on Aspen’s face alone is scaring me. How did you know I was here?”

Karm turns around and looks at me. “Legend got a text and he said let’s go. He’s been acting strange the last couple of days. You know sleeping over and not going home. He hasn’t said anything, but I think something is going on.”

I look over and Journi is extremely quiet. We haven’t spoken since the night of the grill out. I give Karm the eyes motioning for her to say something to Journi. I knew if I said something, she wasn't going to answer me. We have sisterly love, but she can hold a grudge forever. Two years ago, we didn't speak for three months. It drove our mother crazy. Karm catches on to my hint.

"Journi, how has Mecca been acting? Has he said anything?"

"Not any different. Wait that's not true. The other night he came over and we talked and kept promising me he would take care of me. Then he said he had business to handle and wouldn't be back for a few days. But before that, I haven't seen him to tell if something was wrong. He and I are in a weird space." She looks at me, rolls her eyes and folds her arms.

My intention wasn't to break them up. I was angry that night. I wanted Journi to keep herself out of my love life. The things I said was true about her going to Bayden, but I should have never said them in front of Mecca. That's her truth. She has to tell it. "I'm sorry sis."

"It's a little too late."

"I admit I said what I said, and I shouldn't have said it in front of him."

"You're damn right. You shouldn't have said anything."

"Don't come at me like that. You know how you do."

"Yes, I know exactly how I've done in the past. My life is not up for your judgement."

"Oh, but it was okay for you to try and put me and Aspen together?"

"I was trying to help you get out of your own way and see that he cares about you. But I wasn't screaming your business across the yard for everyone to hear. How the hell would you feel if I stood out there and yelled to everyone that Bella has commitment issues. She'll continue to fuck anything that moves because she can't trust a man again."

Sister or not I was going to pop her in the face for saying that to me. But Karm got between us.

"Both of you calm down. This is not the time or the place. Journi you were wrong."

"See I told you!" I was jumping up and down behind Karm, laughing. Until she turned around and looked at me.

"Your ass was wrong too! I swear both of you drive me crazy. I don't know how mom did it. Both of you apologize."

I wasn't about to say anything. She can't tell me what to do.

"I will kick both of your asses in here. Try me if you want that. Apologize!"

I knew Karm was serious. I've fought her too many times and lost. I was not about to do it tonight. Journi and I look at each other. "I'm sorry."

"Yeah, yeah. I'm sorry too!"

"Journi don't be like that. She said she was sorry."

"I get it. But the damage is done. Right now, there are two men in your lives that made sure you were safe and brought you here. I got brought here by someone that works for them. Tonight, you'll feel safe laid up next to your men. I won't. He hasn't even called to check on me. Not even a text. Bella, you took that from me. And as much as I love you. I'm still mad with you."

I walk up to her and hug her. I didn't mean to ruin what she had going for her. How could Mecca just step aside and let Bayden win her back. If he wasn't willing to fight for my sister than he doesn't deserve her. I wasn't about to say that to her. I don't want her in here crying. "Maybe he's just handling something. Give him time. But not too much. We Fields are never just sitting around waiting on a man. On any man." When I hear her giggle, I let her go.

"Now that, that's over we need to know what's going on. I told Legend; I didn't want to get mixed up in his life choices."

I look at Bella. "The guys that approached me tonight didn't say anything about Legend. He only mentioned Mecca and Aspen." Before I could say another word, the door opens. Aspen comes back in.

"Ladies, I know you have questions. I just don't have any answers. But we're on it. For your safety I'm going to have a few of my top men to watch over you. They'll go with you to work and home."

I look at him like he's crazy. "What are you crazy? I can't have security following me around at my job."

"Well than you'll need to take off. And that goes for the rest of you. If Mecca, Legend and I can't have eyes on you, we won't know you're safe. Until we know what's going on, we need to do this." Bella was about to say something. But Aspen's eyes got cold and serious. "It's not up for discussion. Someone will come and escort you to the conference room. They'll order some food. Once we sweep your house, I'll send you all home."

His words were loud and clear. He walks over and kisses me on my cheek and walks out the room. "Damn, he's sexy when he takes control." Journi and Karm give me a crazy look. "What? He is."

Chapter 19

That's All in The Past

Mecca

Alexa play. . .Heather Hunter. . . In My Mind

The smell of New York doesn't change. It smells like blood, sweat and money. I love it. Smells like home to me. I wish I was coming here under different circumstances but that's not the case. I told Journi I would take her with me on the next trip home. She's only been here on a visit. Seeing New York with tourist eyes is different than seeing it through a New Yorker's eyes. I want to show her where I grew up, my favorite place to eat, and where I used to kill it on the courts out here. I want to take her to a Broadway show, show her the real art galleries out here. I know she would love it. Just as the New York breeze hits me, I come to senses and realize I may never get a chance to do any of those things with her. Although she's sent me a few text messages. I know she's still texting that clown. I won't chase her no matter how much I care for her.

I head toward my area of the city, the Bronx. I want to make sure I'm strapped before this meeting. I don't want to take any chances. Although, Hunter knows not try anything. But it's Hunter. That bitch is crazy enough to try it. I met Hunter about five years ago. She's beautiful, smart and successful. We dated off and on for a few months before we started getting heavy into each other. She was the type that didn't require all my time but gave enough of her attention to still make me feel like a man. Thinking back on it she was a good sales agent. She sold me that good woman shit and I brought it hook line and sinker. I trusted her with my life. We were like Bonnie and Clyde. I had her back and she had mine. She knew about some of the business I had going on. She didn't know every detail. She knew enough to know I wasn't a boy scout. When I received a contract to kill a few people and one of them was a friend. I was conflicted and just needed to talk about it. I laid my dilemma on her. I trusted her to keep it open and honest with me. She listened without judgement. Gave me her opinion and helped me decide. I found out later it was all part of her game. She was only listening to gain information. Two weeks after I killed everyone I was placed in cuffs and taken in by the FBI. They knew everything about me. They knew my full background, even things that were off the records. Things only someone close would know. After they questioned me for eight hours about the killings and I didn't break. Hunter walked through the door with her badge on her hip and her FBI jacket on. To say I was shocked, is in understatement. She sat across from me and looked at me like I never had her body twisted in every position in the world. Like I never shared my dreams with her. She sat quietly across from me and pulled out a file she had on me complete with pictures and ticket stubs to every event I had taken her to over the year. I didn't care about any of it. I knew in my heart she was on my side. I knew no matter what line of work she was in she was still mine because her eyes always told me they love me. The difference was the woman sitting in front of me, looked at me like I was the scum of earth. There was a hatred and disgust in her for me. There was no love in them. I was tricked by someone who I thought loved me. She was one hell of an actress, who was damn good at her job.

Because of her I sat in jail for months while the feds tried to build a case against me. They could never get anything solid. When my lawyer finally got them to agree to set bail for me, I went to work digging up everything on Hunter. By the time I was done I knew everything about her, her family, her friends and that I was her chance at getting the promotion she'd been working so hard to get. I wasn't mad that she was trying to advance her career. I was upset she was using me. The good thing about a person that uses people is they always have a long path behind them of upset people they've used along the way. That was no different for her. Hunter's career climb created a slew of enemies and mistakes. She cut a lot of corners to get everything she wanted. I found every enemy, every mistake, every piece of dirty on her and confronted her with it. The next week all the charges were dropped against me. After that happened, she wanted to come back into my life with the excuse that she was never going to testify against me. That she was only going forward with the plan to put on a show for everyone. She claimed her devotion was always to me. It was lies. I knew it. She was only coming back because she lost the promotion and her pride was on the line. I had turned the tables on her, and she didn't like it. All the time she spent with me she chose to only see the gentle side not the hardcore street side. Unfortunately, by the time she saw it fully, she was on the receiving end. To know my thug ass got the best of her just didn't sit right. That's when I saw her other side. She went bat shit crazy. She stalked my every move. Every person I let into my life after that she found a way to get in between me and them. She would make random pop-ups in my life. I had to threaten to kill her and something that she loved, to get her to stay out of my life. And now here I am inviting her back. Giving her access to me once again. Everything in me knew this was wrong. But I needed to get the information. I knew she wasn't after us. But she had the resources to know who is.

I watch the black car with dark tinted windows pull up and park. She gets out and still looks flawlessly beautiful. But I knew that was only on the outside. I know enough about Hunter to know on the inside, she's a nasty, dirty, ugly bitch. A smile crosses her lips when our eyes make contact.

"I knew time would only age you into something even better than before."

She runs up to me and hugs me. I don't return it; I just stand there. "You look the same Hunter. I'm glad your outside doesn't reflect what's on the inside of you."

"Your compliments have turned to crap. I remember when you couldn't stop telling me how beautiful I am. Am I not beautiful any more Mecca?"

She steps back and twirls around like a little kid. The outfit she has on leaves little to the imagination. But I don't need to imagine. She could stand in front of me completely naked and it would do nothing for me. A woman can be drop dead gorgeous, but her bite could be as poisonous as a scorpion. It's her bite that I know will kill me. "You're still you Hunter. Let's get down to business."

"You got a new bitch Mecca? Yeah, you do. I can see it in your face. Who is she? Do you love her? You can't love her because you promised to love only me. And she can't replace me. I'm irreplaceable. Mecca?"

I knew she would get off track. She has this bewildered look in her eyes. "I need to know who is investigation me and my people? It is you again? Because you know if it is." That last statement snaps her back into the conversation.

"I wouldn't do that to you again. I promised. And you promised."

"I know what I promised. I know what I agreed to do. But someone has opened a case. If it's not you, who it is?"

"I don't know. No one in my office."

"Find out who. You have twenty-four hours."

"Okay. I'll find out. If I do. Will you reward me?"

"I won't play these games with you. Get me what I need or else." I turn and walk away. I hate dealing with her crazy ass. Just to make sure she stays on task I'll have someone watch her.

The next morning sitting eating breakfast in my apartment Journi crosses my mind. That last visit with her felt like it was our last together. I couldn't shake that feeling and its fucking with me. I spoke with Aspen last night and he told me about bringing the ladies in the office for their own protection. Just hearing that Bella was in danger made me ready to be back in Atlanta. We have some of the best men on our security team watching her and her sisters, but none of them can protect her like I can. I had to shake those thoughts out of my mind. I have moves to make and leads to follow. I wasn't about to trust Hunter to get me the full story. I could give her crazy ass a box of crayons to color a picture and she would only use one color. I need to see the full picture.

I hit the street and it feels like I'm walking back in time. When I was hemmed up on charges years ago, I had to do the same thing I'm doing now. The only difference is back then I was covering my tracks. This time I'm protecting the people around me. My first stop is to see some mutual associates, that I've known since growing up. I had already hit Pharaoh up to let him know I would be in town. I head straight for his office where him, King and I have a meeting set up. Pharaoh and King have the city of New York on lock when it comes down to law enforcement agencies. They have pretty much everyone in their pocket.

"Man, Pharaoh, I think I need a refund. I thought you made my office look good, but this right here is unbelievable." I could tell that no expense was spared designing his office. From the murals on the wall, to the art pieces down to the marble floors nothing in here was bought out of a store or off the shelf.

"You got to watch him Mecca, that's what he does. Takes people's money and uses it to upgrade his office."

I laugh and dap up King and Pharaoh. "It's good to see you both."

"What's up with you? How is the new office space? Do I need to change anything? I got an order in the other day to fix some glass. Did my men mess up? We'll fix it right away."

I couldn't work for Pharaoh. He seems all nice and harmless, but he's a beast in the office and in the streets. I've heard a lot of stories about his workers disappearing if they messed up his designed. Paige has calmed him down, but I guess he's like me, when that itch comes up you have to scratch it. "That wasn't your workers, that was Legend's ass. You know he's a damn hot head. I gave him the news about everything going on and he went off in there. Breaking up all my new shit. Aspen told me not to bring him in there."

"Your ass hard-headed. You been knew his ass was crazy. He's not going to like everything we found out. Pharaoh, told me right after meeting Swiss he didn't like him. My brother is crazy but he's always right about people. You know I cut some ties with Legend behind Swiss. He thought he was out here running things. Every time Legend turned his head or went out of town, Swiss was there making changes and fucking things up. I had to put him in his place more than a few times. It was on the strength of my friendship with Legend I didn't kill him."

I listen as King breaks down everything for me. I've learned street records, which is really word of mouth, transmits better if you go directly to the source. I can pull up someone's criminal history, their family history and all types of reports. But what you do on the streets will override everything. The streets will tell you the truth about a person if you get it from the right source. Either you are loved and respected or you are grimy and dirty. Swiss is as dirty as they come. Legend doesn't know the kind of backroom deals Swiss has made in his name. Swiss has been using Legend's name like they are married. He's been shopping around getting credit off the strength of everything Legend has done. When he's done Pharaoh looks at me with a serious face. That could only mean one thing. "Who put a hit out on me?"

"No hit. King nor I would ever take a contract on our friends. I've seen Hunter around. She's been searching for you hard. I think she's gotten even crazier than before. I didn't even think that was possible. I've seen her with Swiss. They've tried to hide it, but I heard some rumors. I went to check it myself. Saw it with my own eyes. I know how you feel—"

"Felt!"

"I know how you felt about her but don't let that snake slither back into your life. She's no good. And him and her are up to something. Mark my words."

Leaving King and Pharaoh's office I felt like my world had been rocked. I gave Hunter a pass years ago because I was in love with her. It didn't matter that she twisted my heart and tossed it in a basket to further her career. What mattered was what we shared. Deep down inside I want to believe she's the girl I fell head over heels for, but I know she's not. Instead of going back to my apartment I head over to the hotel and text Hunter to meet me there. She wants to play games. Let's play.

Chapter 20

The Good and the Bad

Journi

Alexa play. . . Kehlani feat. August. . . Nunya

I've been in the house for three days. I feel like the walls are closing in on me. Unlike my sisters I didn't have a job to go to each day. That left me home doing absolutely nothing. Unless I could call phone watching, a job. The past three days I hadn't received not one phone call or text from Mecca. Only messages from him through Legend and Aspen. And I didn't believe he was sending them. I think they felt sorry for me. They were just trying to help me save face. They didn't need to do it. I understood. I messed up by not telling him. But he jumped the gun by assuming. Maybe we both didn't know how to communicate clearly to one another. I thought we were better after the night he came over.

It was quiet in the house. I could see the rays from the sun shining through the blinds. I position myself on the part of the sofa that would allow the sun rays to touch my face. The warmth of it feels good. I close my eyes. I can see Mecca's face. His smile that chocolate skin of his and those dimples. I'm taken back to the day he and I woke up in bed together and stayed that way the entire day. He was laying on his stomach with his arms hanging over the bed tapping away on his laptop. I was peeping over his shoulders, pretending like I was trying to see what he was doing. I wasn't. I just wanted his attention. He kept saying to give him five more minutes. I occupied my time by tracing all the tattoos on him first with my fingertips and then with my tongue. I made sure I kissed all his scars that I happened upon on the way to the next area of his body. I kept thinking I was obsessed with him. I had to be because I couldn't keep my hands off of him. I would lay my head on his back and listen to his heartbeat like it was music. Music that made my soul feel at peace. My phone ringing snapped me back to where I was at the moment. All the warmth and peace I was feeling was snapped right out of me too. I suck my teeth and pick up the phone without looking at who was calling me. "Hello."

"You finally picked up for me."

I sit up abruptly at the sound of his voice. I want to kick myself for not checking to see who was calling me. "Hey Bayden."

"Come on Journi. I miss you baby. You have to miss just a little."

"I don't."

"You're just saying that because you're still angry and I understand. But I meant everything I've been saying to you. I'm going to make everything up to you. How about you meet me for lunch? Before you say no. It's just lunch. I promise that's it."

This was the moment I've been waiting on. The moment he would call me and be sincere about talking with me. Talking over our options. "Text me the location and I'll meet you there."

"Yes, baby I promise you won't regret it."

When I hang up, my first thought is to lay back down and go back to the world I was daydreaming about with Mecca. But I couldn't. I can't live in a dream. I live in the real world. I pass by the window and I see the guys outside standing guard. I can't just walk out the front door they'll see me. I'll need to go through the back door. I walk upset to shower and change.

Hopping the fence in the backyard was crazy. I feel like I was a teenager all over again sneaking out the house to go to a party. Back then it was more fun. Now it's just silly. I know if I walked through the front door Aspen's security guy would follow me and report back to him, I went to meet a man. I didn't want that getting back to Mecca. A few blocks away my Uber is waiting for me. I hop in and tuck my purse close to me. I made sure to bring my gun just in case.

Instead of Bayden opting for something nice and quiet he picked Pappadeauxs. It's one of my favorite places but not something I was in the mood for today. I spot him standing next to a group of women smiling. I see nothing really changes with him. I walk over and make sure he knows I could care less about the women next to him. "Hey, it looks like you are busy. Do you want to go somewhere else?" He pulls me in and hugs me.

"You look beautiful. You know I love when your hair is straight like that. We can stay here. They should be calling us pretty soon. But it's up to you. If you're not happy with this, we can go somewhere else."

"No this is fine." He finds us a spot under the tree to sit and wait for our table.

"I'm glad you agreed to come out and meet me today. You look good."

He gets closer to me and kisses me on my neck. I simply smile. This is his thing. He doesn't bring flowers or candy; he brings his charm. Once we are seated at the table, he orders for both of us. I hate that he does that. He always wants to think and control me. "You know I can order for myself."

"I know, I just want to show you that I know you. That I remember everything you like. I miss you Journi. I know everything between us wasn't perfect but what we had was beautiful. I want you to come back to home. I miss walking into the house smelling your delicious cooking and seeing your beautiful face."

What he means to say is fussing at me for cooking too much food and reminding me how I'm supposed to be on a diet. "Bayden, you don't mean any of that at all. You hated my cooking. You were always on me about cooking the wrong meal because my fat ass needed to lose some weight. Those were your words not mine."

"That's not true."

"You just ordered me a grilled chicken salad."

"I ordered you something you like. Besides there's nothing wrong with me wanting you to be healthy. I care about you. I was just trying to be helpful."

The waiter comes over with a special plate with a cover over it. Bayden smiles. "What's this?" He lifts the top and under it is a small ring box.

"I got you something nice. You deserve it. Go ahead open it."

I take the cover and place it back over the plate. "The reason I came to meet with you today is because I want out. I want out of everything that was in my name. I want out of everything that has us twisted up together. I didn't come here because I want to be back with you." He sits back and stares at me for a minute.

"I bring your ass to a nice restaurant. I order you some good food. I get you these expensive as diamond earrings that you don't even bother to look at."

"There's no need to look at them. They are just another *I'm sorry* gift to add to all the others I have from you. I don't want it."

He bangs his hand on the table. "Stop it Journi."

"No, you stop it. You come here with your fakeness and gifts, telling me how much you miss me. It's bullshit. You just miss the control you had over me. You miss me waiting on you hand and foot. You miss me taking you back after you fuck over me time and time again. Not this time. I don't want your gifts. I don't want your fake apologies. You can save them for the little bitch you've been playing house with out in Miami. I just want you take my name off of everything. I don't want any more ties to you or with you."

"And the money?"

"You can have it. I'll give it back once I know you have removed me from everything."

"Why now? Tell me it's not for that nigga I saw you with at the house. We both know we visit the hood to play and fuck them. We don't adjust to their levels. We're above them. Have I taught you nothing? You still playing hood games."

"What he and I have is none of your business. I just want out."

"Tell me why! I've done too much for you over the years. I deserve more than you wanting out."

I look him straight in his eyes. "I love him. Is that what you want to hear? He treats me better, he's good for me and he fucks me better." He wanted to know. Now he knows. I love Mecca but I couldn't be with him with fully I until I completely cut ties with Bayden. Mecca is like a dream come true. He treats me good. He accepts me for who I am. He hasn't tried to change me. And it's true no man has fucked me the way he does. I don't want to lose him. That's why I've been playing nice to Bayden. Trying to get him to release me from my responsibility in his mess. But I see he's not going to do it. No matter how nice I ask.

"Fucks you good huh. My bitch in Miami fucks me better than you anyway. She doesn't just lay there. She's good at making me money like you use to do. No one walks away from me not even you Journi. This is over. Pay for this shit yourself."

He gets up and walks away from the table. I take that ring box and throw it at his head. I wish it was something bigger and harder to knock him out. I don't know what to do now. When I saw the papers on Mecca's desk, I knew he was looking into Bayden's company. I know he's going to find out everything. He's going to find out everything about me too.

I stand out front wanting on my Uber. As the thoughts of Mecca knowing all the dirty things, I agreed to do with Bayden runs through my mind, my phone rings. "Hello."

"Journi where are you?"

"I'm home."

"Don't lie to me. I'm here at your house. Where are you?"

"Mecca, I'm sorry I'm not the person you think I am. I've done a lot of things I'm not proud of and I was just trying to fix it and make it right." I was babbling on and on when I hear tires screeching. I hear gun shots and before I could duck down, I feel a bullet going through my body. When I hit the ground, I drop my phone and I can hear Mecca screaming. I feel the concrete under me. People are standing over me screaming. But I can't see their faces. I just see my mom's face. I focus on her opening her arms for me. I've been making myself sick holding everything inside. I didn't want to feel the pain anymore. I just need her to hold me and tell me everything will be okay. I run into them and break down crying.

To Be Continued

Bio

Nola Jewels, is a New Orleans native who currently resides in Georgia. Growing up in New Orleans, reading became an escape from the reality surrounding her. A love of reading lead to her developing a passion for writing short stories, poetry and works of fiction. Writing and developing her own stories became not only an outlet but a gift. A gift that has grown into an amazing ability to create unique, Urban Tales. Nola introduced herself to the world with her first book When A Boss Loves You; Pharaoh & Paige. The book was a combination of her poetry and her ability to create characters who pull and tug at your heart. Her ability to fill her stories with drama, twisted with romance and suspense, topped with erotica creates a perfect gumbo that leaves readers filled up and wanting more. Nola plans to continue writing and sharing her gift of sensual, loving, honest and, unapologetic stories.

Stay in contact:

Facebook: https://www.facebook.com/nola.jewels.35

Instagram: https://instagram.com/nolajewels_author

Twitter: https://twitter.com/jewels_nola

Join the *Dripping in Jewels* Facebook readers group for special sneak peeks:
https://www.facebook.com/groups/366028187559572/

A Savage Set My Soul on Fire

Synopsis

The life that Lacye Samuels has had to endure has been nothing short of heartbreaking. The abuse she's experienced from her mother and stepdad has left her sheltered and guarded. Her only motivation is to one day escape the darkness that surrounds her. Her vision is clear: work hard, get an education and walk away from the house of horrors for good. When the opportunity to get more money comes her way she jumps at the chance. Money is now her goal and the path she's taking to get it will lead her down the road to an unexpected future.

The Hampton brothers Za'Shon 'Fire', Jaivon, and Tyree are running things in Atlanta. Of the trio, Fire's the most arrogant and the only one willing to do anything to take his family to the next level. His focus was on one thing building his empire and making more money. That is until he meets Lacye. He falls fast for her.

Lacye has never met someone like Fire. He's arrogance and bluntness takes her by surprise. But it's also the thing she falls in love with. He believes he's found the perfect woman who's beautiful, smart, and innocent. Their romance goes fast but the secrets she's been holding comes out. His lifestyle and her secrets crash together making the perfect storm. It leaves a path of destruction and hurt. They both find themselves losing everything they've worked so hard for. Za'Shon won't allow his world to come crashing down and he won't lose Lacye. The savage in him won't let her go but the cost of loving her threatens to bring down him and his brothers. His recklessness creates havoc and starts a war that threatens to take everything and everyone away from him. But that's what happens when you set Fire to Lacye.

Completed Series Available on Amazon

CPSIA information can be obtained
at www.ICGtesting.com
Printed in the USA
LVHW081245281220
675097LV00019B/1526

9 798557 250139